Dear Entitled Hotel Guests,

By Deenie Luckie

Dear Entitled Hotel Guests,
By Deenie Luckie

ISBN-13: 979-8-218-23443-0
Copyright 2023 @ Deenie Luckie

Manufactured in the United States of America

Dear Entitled Hotel Guests

For my daughter; Jelani, and her grandmother; Naderah.

Spring

Check In 1
The Garden Tree Lakeside Resort..............15
Management...25
Let the Shenanigans Begin..........................45

Summer

The Garden of Flower.................................59
Dirty Laundry..71
Housekeeping...83
Sports 93
Weddings..105
Things People Say...................................*122*

Autumn

Autumn and the Leaf Peepers......................125
Hotel vs Airbnb...137
Jewel Vacations Alone 141

Winter

Hockey 161
Winter..173
Reviews..185
The End..197
Jewel Checks In 203
Stinger...207
Hotel & Sports Trivia **210**

SPRING

Check In

It's 1:58 p.m. on a rainy afternoon. Jewel looks out the window and sees a strike of lightning in the sky with the roaring sounds of thunder following along. She's at home sulking while getting dressed for work. She dreads going out in the rain. She would rather stay home, watching a movie and eating something she has no business eating, like a pint of Ben n Jerry's butter pecan ice cream with a side of Lay's classic potato chips. The sweet, salty, and nutty combination has Jewel's tongue in a twist. Instead of accommodating her desire for junk food, she grabs an umbrella out of the closet and heads out the door.

A few blocks later, she's at work.

Clock in: 3:00 p.m.

Check in time starts: 4:00 p.m.

A tall, White attractive man approaches the counter, dressed in a blue suit, looking as if he just got off of work.

"Good afternoon, Sir," Jewels says. "How are you doing today?"

"I'm doing well. Thank you."

"Are you here to check in?"

"Yes, I am."

"May I have your last name please?" Jewel asks.

"Mr. Whitlock."

"Give me one second to get your registration sheet."

"Okay."

Jewel retrieves his registration sheet paper clipped to a postcard sized parking pass. She places the sheet on top of the counter in front of Mr. Whitlock. She holds onto the parking pass as she begins the longest check in process in hotel history.

"Please confirm your name and address are correct. May I have your car make and model, your license plate, and your best contact number? If your email address is correct, you do not have to repeat it." She points to different spots in the body of the registration sheet. "Please initial, initial, initial: First, there is no smoking in the hotel. A $500.00 fine is applied if smoking is discovered in the room."

"We don't smoke."

"That's great!" Jewel acknowledges before she continues. "Second, the gym and the pool are open every day from 6:00 a.m. to 10:00 p.m. However, there is no lifeguard on duty in the pool area. Third, are you aware of traveling during the CoronaVirus Pandemic? If anyone in your party comes down with a fever and test positive for the virus please inform the front desk. This way we can take precautions within our housekeeping department. Finally, may I please have your signature?"

Mr. Whitlock takes a minute to review. He completes the registration sheet.

On the parking pass with a large black marker, Jewel writes Mr. Whitlock's name and the expiration date, which is his checkout date.

Mr. Whitlock hands the registration sheet over to Jewel.

"Thank you."

She enters all the information collected on the registration sheet into the computer system using the application, Hotel Master.

"Mr. Whitlock, how many keys would you like for your room?"

"Two is fine."

Jewel programs the keys to synchronize with the room before picking up a key packet from the side of the computer. She slides the keys into the packet, picks up a black marker, and writes the room number on the front.

She also hands Mr. Whitlock the parking pass.

"Please put the parking pass in the dashboard of your car and the best parking garage for your room is garage A."

"How do I get to parking garage A?"

"Behind you, pass the elevators, down the hallway. Take the stairwell on your right. Go down one flight of steps and you'll be in parking garage A."

"Thank you. How do I get to my room?"

"Your keys are inside the packet."

She shows him the key packet, flipping it open into a map. "This is a map of the hotel. Your room number is 34." Jewel locates the guest's assigned room and the parking garage on the map. Then she turns the packet over. "These are your Wi-Fi instructions."

"Thank you for all your help!"

"Please enjoy your stay, Mr. Whitlock. My name is Jewel. If you have any questions dial 0 for the front desk and someone will be happy to assist you."

"Thank you."

"You're welcome, good evening."

"Good evening," says Mr. Whitlock.

And he walks away.

In her spill, Jewel excludes the housekeeping tidy service

offered. It can be a hit or miss. She doesn't like it when a guest approaches her station saying that she told them they'll receive housekeeping service, and then housekeeping is a no show. So, she opts out of that part of the spill.

That's how Jewel's first check in of the day should start. But then the twist, turns, and the shenanigans of the second shift begins. Jewel is a Front Desk Clerk at a three-star hotel in Upstate NY. The second shift is 3:00 p.m. - 11:00 p.m. Elizabeth, Brenda, and Jewel work the second shift.

Elizabeth has been working with the Garden Tree Lakeside Resort for four years. Brenda and Jewel are just beginning their employment with the hotel. Jewel is one week ahead of Brenda.

Elizabeth is also known as the Upgrade Queen. She's a fifty-eight year old, tall, blonde, overweight, White American woman, originally from NJ. She has been living in Upstate, NY, since she was eighteen years old. She's married with five adult children. She's a kind lady who would give you the shirt off her back.

She has a forty-five minute commute from the resort to her house. Elizabeth lives in a rural area with horses, goats, and cows as her neighbors. She lives next door to her adult disabled daughter, Linda. She helps care for Linda.

Elizabeth will tell you she doesn't have any patience but she works well with people. She just doesn't have much patiences for rowdy entitled hotel guests. For additional income, she works in the mornings as a health aid employee, working with the elderly.

She attends church on Sundays when she is not at work. She and her husband contribute to the community with cookies, cakes and yard sales, and she enjoys decorating the town during the holiday.

Elizabeth is always in the bosses' office, but she expresses how others spend too much time in the bosses' office. She has a routine each day when she arrives at work. She sets her station up for the evening shift by making sure everything is stocked. She'll check to make sure the clear, glass jars that sit on the granite countertop are filled with pens, and the coffee and creamer bins are full for the shift. Complimentary coffee, creamer, soap, shampoo, and lots of other items are kept behind the front desk for guests. After she has confirmed all guests have been taken care of she heads to the bosses' office.

Staff members have expressed their dislike for Elizabeth. They say she can't be trusted. Jewel has witnessed Elizabeth sharing a confidential text between her and another staff member with the bosses.

Elizabeth was heading into the bosses' office as a part of her routine. Jewel walked over to the coffee and tea station for hot water and overheard Elizabeth telling the bosses about a text between her and Joe, one of the housemen.

Joe was not getting paid for one reason or another. He texts Elizabeth through Facebook complaining that his rent and car payment are late because the Human Resource Manager has not paid him. In the Facebook text, he asked Elizabeth not to share their text with anyone.

Jewel is listening to Elizabeth tell management all this information. She heads back to her station with her hot water in hand. She keeps quiet about what she heard and goes about her evening.

The next evening while Brenda and Jewel are working. Joe comes to the front desk, angry and complaining to them.

He explains how management confronted him about the text between him and Elizabeth. "She was yelling at me and pointing her fingers in my face. Then she said, 'You know Joe, if you have an issue with the way I'm running things around here, make sure you come to me first! I don't appreciate you sending those text messages to Elizabeth.' She acts as if she's better than me," Joe cries.

Now Joe is going around the hotel bad mouthing Elizabeth. He thought she was his friend and so his feelings are hurt.

The first shift front desk clerks are asking Jewel what's going on. She replied to everyone with the same response.

"Maybe Joe is looking for a friend to be on his side. Like a I-hate-Elizabeth fan club. I really don't know. Hopefully he'll move on from this drama soon."

Brenda chimes in, "Well, I'm not the biggest fan of Elizabeth myself. She's always in people's business. The reason for all this drama in the first place. Joe had no business texting her. What made him think she was his friend is beyond me."

Elizabeth is stationed at the far right of the front desk. She is the first front desk clerk a guest sees when the resort's double door opens.

When Jewel is not working with Elizabeth, she's working with Brenda.

Brenda's a thirty-two year old, small, large breasted, Black American woman. She has a beautiful cocoa complexion. She wears her hair in a cute baby bun. She's from Los Angeles, California. She has a boyfriend, Tanner, who works security during busy nights. They've been together for five years. They have the cutest relationship. You can tell how much he loves her. They travel throughout the United States as if they're nomads, from California to Alaska, Idaho, Utah, and other states. The front desk gets to hear all the stories of their travels.

Brenda laughs and laughs and laughs all day. No, reasons behind it, it's just non-stop laughing. So much to the point that it's weird. She likes to brag about all the money she's made throughout her travels from being a waitress or a restaurant manager.

Her and Tanner stumbled upon Upstate, NY. They liked it and decided to set up roots. Brenda is stationed in the center when the three of them are working together. Elizabeth questions Brenda's honesty about some of her stories. She says Brenda exaggerates everything she says. She feels it's difficult to believe anything she tells us. Jewel listens and doesn't say much. Jewel understands where Elizabeth is coming from.

The three ladies are working together this evening. While softly laughing, Brenda tells them she used to make $30-$50 per hour as a waitress. They're just listening. Her eyes are facing Jewel's direction while she is speaking. Jewel is standing looking at them. Elizabeth is looking at Jewel shaking her head while rolling her eyes in disbelief of anything Brenda is saying.

"I'm not sure the waiters are making that kind of money here," Elizabeth says.

When Brenda steps away to the restroom, Elizabeth starts to question Jewel.

"If it's true what Brenda is saying, why is she working at the front desk of a hotel instead of working in the local restaurant?" Jewel doesn't want to get involved, mainly because she just doesn't care.

She nods at Elizabeth and says, "I don't know, Elizabeth."

Elizabeth likes a little bit of drama. Jewel believes the drama adds spice to Elizabeth's life.

Jewel is fifty-one years old, 5 ft. 4 inches tall, 135 lb. single Black American woman from NYC. She has two adult female children, Randy and Jolly. Both girls live in NYC, but she doesn't have a relationship with Randy. Jolly and Jewel are like twins. They see each other every six months.

Jewel lives a quiet, lonely life, and enjoys traveling. Her favorite destination is the Caribbean. She helps take care of her mother who has dementia. Jewel's mother, Nala, lives in an independent senior apartment building. It's a nice place, within walking distance to Jewel's apartment. She tries to visit Nala once a week. She is a small, short lady, who sits at home watching television and reading a book everyday. She is not very social but she'll go outside everyday to walk to the store.

Jewel moved Upstate to create a better life for herself. Upon arrival at the picturesque lakeside resort town, she settled on a one bedroom apartment on Mirror Lake for $950.00 a month. Moving from Hell's Kitchen, NYC that's a steal, especially for living on a lake. It's a shotgun style apartment. The kitchen/bathroom, dining area, living room area, and then the bedroom line up in that order of the apartment.

The bedroom has a large window overlooking Mirror Lake. The mountain's reflections on the lake are so clear on nice days. The reason for the name Mirror Lake. There is so much beauty, peace, and calm living in all this nature. The only noise she hears on the lake are the sounds of ducks quacking.

With a commercial storefront for rent above her apartment, and a dream to start her own business, it was a double win for her. The feeling of excitement and blessings overwhelmed her. The storefront commercial unit rented for $2,400.00 per month. Again, Jewel thought this was a steal. Now, she had to secure the funding for the business. A health food store for this area would be perfect for the sports driven community. She goes to the local bank and inquires about funding for the health food store. She works on the business plan. She gets her finances in order. She's assigned a caseworker, Steve. A sweet man who helps her with the paperwork to be approved with the state. There's a process before approval. For example, a credit check and making sure ten percent of the funding toward the business was in her bank account.

Jewel opened the health food store, January 2020. Five weeks later, she had to shut it down due to the CoronaVirus Pandemic. The new business was shut down for six weeks before reopening.

Four months later, the town went through a complete rehab. A huge construction project on Main Street that included new granite sidewalks, plumbing, and street pavement. A two-year construction project that crushed the business.

The health food store went out of business after two years of blood and sweat. It would have survived had it not been for the high rent that Jewel thought was a steal. How ironic.

It was time to find a job. That's how Jewel began to work at the Garden Tree Lakeside Resort. She's stationed to the far left of the front desk counter.

The Garden Tree Lakeside Resort is located in Lake Avid, NY, a small village located in the Adirondack Mountains. There's a population of 2,300 people living in the village year round. It is engulfed within 360 degrees of mountain views. Famous for its winter sports events; for example, hockey and skiing.

Lake Avid experiences four true seasons. With recreational

activities offered each season, [well...Mud season may be questionable.] People come from all over the world to enjoy the winter wonderland the area has created. A bobsled run at Mount Van Hoevenberg, skiing at Whiteface Mountain, a ten-foot ski jump, and more. A playground for the rich and famous to relax all while breathing fresh mountain air.

The first shift, aka shift one, or as Jewel would say: the sick shift. This shift is always sick and passes along their germs throughout the hotel. Mary, Stella (the main carrier of the germs), and Gilligan (AKA the rat) work shift one.

Mary is the sweetest young White American woman from the area. She's a sensitive young lady. From time to time she will break down crying from the large number of rude and entitled people that pass through the hotel's lobby. She lives at home with her father and dog. Mary has a boyfriend.

Jewel arrives for her shift before Mary heads out and she approaches Jewel.

"Jewel I have some news I want to share with you before anyone else tells you."

Jewel is listening intensely.

"Sure, what's up?"

"I'm pregnant."

"Wow, congratulations Mary! How exciting is that? Did

you tell management?

"I will soon. I know they can't afford for me to take three months off for maternity leave."

"They'll figure it out before you leave." Jewel proceeds to give Mary a hug. "Congratulations again Mary, I'm very happy for you."

"Thank you, Jewel. I'm nervous."

"You'll be okay, sweetie. Let me know whenever you want to chat. I'm here for you."

"Thank you. I'm heading out now. I'll see you tomorrow."

"Okay, good night."

Mary exits the front desk station area and heads home.

The Garden Tree Lakeside Resort

E lizabeth and Jewel are on shift this evening. The hotel lobby is quiet. The ladies are standing at their stations pondering, while staring out the window. An older model brown Range Rover SUV is driving towards the front door and has parked. A handsome, young, bald, White man gets out the Range Rover. He has on a black sweat suit and looks as if he's ready for a vacation. He's alone. He approaches the oakwood, double automatic doors and enters into the foyer. The foyer walls are oakwood with a large, colorful area rug on the floor.

The handsome man is looking straight ahead standing in front of a large, framed painting of the snowy mountainside. The painting offers a vibe of tranquility and serenity. He continues onward, through another set of oakwood double doors with a glass pane. Looking straight ahead through those doors is the front desk station.

Elizabeth is the first front desk clerk to be seen upon arrival. She is straight ahead once the double door opens, so she checks in most of the guests.

Once the handsome man catches his bearings from being in awe of the lobby's large picturesque floor-to-ceiling windows overlooking Mirror Lake. He proceeds to Elizabeth's station. It is breathtaking to be engulfed in the large space. With a vaulted ceiling and mid-century styled black metal chandeliers hanging from above, you feel like you have taken a step back in time. The front desk is built out of oakwood, hand carved, shaven of the Adirondack Mountains. A granite counter lays on top of all the oakwood. The front desk staff faces the lobby, front door entryway with an open loft above.

"Good afternoon Sir. How may I help you, Elizabeth asked?"

"Yes, my name is Mr. Hart, I would like to know if my room is available?"

Elizabeth, checks Hotel Master. "Yes, Mr. Hart, your room is ready early. Let's get you settled in. Give me a second while I retrieve your registration sheet."

"Okay, thank you."

Elizabeth returns with a smile.

"Mr. Hart, I see you have booked a Standard Lakeside room."

"Yes, I did."

Elizabeth is typing (tap, tap) while speaking with Mr. Hart. "Well, I do have a Specialty suite available, if you would like, with a fireplace and other amenities. Let me check and see which suites are available. I'll check the prices, too."

Mr. Hart has a smile on his face. He replies, "Yes, please.

That sounds nice, especially on a chilly evening like tonight."

Elizabeth is staring at the computer and communicating to Mr. Hart the availability. "Certainly, you're 100% correct! Well, we just so happen to have the Nippletop suite available. It's like a honeymoon suite with a propane gas fireplace and a jetted tub for soaking. This suite has a heated towel warmer, too. The Nippletop suite will cost you an extra $100.00 for your four-night stay."

Mr. Hart shrugs his shoulders and pouts his lips. "That's not too bad, what other options do you have for me?"

"We have the Nye Suite, a 700 sq. ft. king bedroom overlooking Mirror Lake with a wood burning fireplace, a shower, and a jetted tub. The Nye Suite will cost an additional $75.00 per night."

Mr. Hart's eyes widened with excitement. "I like the idea of a wood burning fireplace. I would like to upgrade to the Nye Suite."

"Thank you, Mr. Hart, let me update your registration sheet." She's excited but remains calm by giving Mr. Hart a big grin.

Elizabeth completes the check in.

He proceeds to walk to the floor-to-ceiling windows, overlooking Mirror Lake. He takes a moment to rest on a second couch resting in front of a propane gas fireplace. He's so handsome Elizabeth and Jewel can't take their eyes off of his every move. There's a coffee table between the couch and the fireplace with end tables on each side of the couch. Mirror Lake is out the window to the left. If you look ahead slightly next to the right, adjacent to the fireplace while sitting on the couch, you can see the bosses' office. Before going into the office to your right there are stairs that lead up into the loft space. The loft space is located on the fourth floor overlooking the lobby with a small library of books. A place where you can sit and read, play a board game, chess, checkers, or play your hand at a deck of cards.

Thanks to Mr. Hart, Elizabeth has just made the hotel some extra cash by upgrading his room. The General Manager rewards her with 15% of the upgrade. An upgrade sheet is posted on the wall in the office behind the front desk counter. The upgrade sheet is numbered 1-25. Each line must include the guest's name, their room number, how much the upgrade was for, and the front desk clerk name who made the sale with their commission amount due posted next to their name.

The upgrade sheet is posted for all staff members to see how much each person is getting paid. This is the reason for Elizabeth's nickname, the Upgrade Queen.

Elizabeth easily takes home an extra two thousand a month in upgrades. It can take a minimum of up to a month to complete the upgrade sheet. Except during hockey time when the front desk staff are restricted from upgrading to these groups of athletes. When hockey events are in town, it can take three or even up to six months to complete an upgrade sheet. Hockey teams are assigned their room a year in advance. With upgrades being paid through a third party for example, CAN/AM.

Elizabeth and Jewel are the only two clerks that participate in the Upgrade program. The other staff members are either too shy, and/or too nervous to participate. They do not have the hustle spirit in them. Jewel had a conversation with Mary about the upgrade program one afternoon before she clocked out.

"Hey, what's so hard about the upgrade program? You're leaving money on the table," Jewel says to Mary.

"I just can't ask people for their money," Mary signs, her shoulder slumped in defeat.

Jewel wants to try and understand the reasoning behind leaving "money on the table."

"I just can't ask people for their money," Mary repeats.

"Mary, it's just letting people know their options. If you're not letting the guest know the different room types at check in, how would they know they had options?"

"It's difficult for me to get the words out of my mouth."

"Don't compare your financial woes with others. You live your life one-way, the guests that stay here live their life differently. Some guests want and can afford luxury. Be brave and get paid."

"You're right, Jewel. I'm going to start practicing at home.

I'll ask my dad to play the guest role for me."

"Now that's a great idea! I know you can do it, Mary. How have you been feeling? You look great!"

Mary has this big grin on her face as she is rubbing on her stomach.

"I'm feeling great. I get a little morning sickness but I guess that should be expected."

"Yes, that does come with being pregnant. It usually lasts the first few months and then you should be fine."

Mary is walking towards the door, heading out.

"Thank you for the chat, Jewel. I appreciate your help. Have a good night."

"Anytime. You too. I'll see you later."

To get an upgrade means you're not only doing your job but it requires you to be brave, Jewel thought. She felt like the other clerks were not doing their job.

If all the front desk staff participated in the upgrade program, the sheet would be completed quickly and they would all get paid faster. Elizabeth saw it a little differently. She was happy without the extra competition. If everyone participated that would leave less inventory for her to sell. Jewel was the type of person who liked to congratulate people instead of hating on them. Jewel wanted everyone to succeed. It was a friendly competition between Elizabeth and Jewel. It was a fun and profitable competition.

The Garden Tree Lakeside Resort is a 170-room hotel. One hundred and ten rooms are Lakeside, forty rooms are Village side which means they are facing the Main Street or parking lot for a view, and twenty rooms are Specialty suites.

The Standard Lakeside room overlooks Mirror Lake and has a king bed or two queen beds, a kitchenette with a mini refrigerator, a Keurig machine with complimentary coffee, and a shower/tub combination.

There are nine different Specialty Suites: named after one of the forty-six High Peak Mountains in the Adirondack, all include a refrigerator and a Keurig machine with coffee. Some suites include jetted tubs, fireplaces, and kitchenettes.

Expanding from the hotel lobby are the guest's rooms in the directions of north and south. Each direction has its own bank of elevators and several stairwells. Each floor has its own ice and vending machine for snacks.

Within the Garden Tree Lakeside Resort there's a restaurant called The Garden of Eden. The Garden of Flower is the resort's spa. The Tree House is the ballroom where the wedding receptions are held. A small shopping center called Devine Mall is where guests can buy souvenirs and coffee. A gym, a pool, a wedding planner, a laundry service, and a housekeeping department are also located on site.

The hallway walls are lined with wallpaper and oakwood chair rail. Carpet floors and simple black chandeliers are centered along the hallway ceilings. The hotel has cameras throughout the building that management watches daily.

The Garden of Eden is run by Ace, a thirty year old, short and slim, gay, White American male, living in the area. A sweet gentleman who always comes to the front desk for a chat.

The Garden of Eden has a large open space filled with dining tables and chairs, a bar, and a kitchen serving standard American food.

The staff gets 50% off meals and drinks at the Garden of Eden. It's a great incentive seeing how expensive food has become. Until you see the health report posted by the Health Department.

Ace has come down for his nightly chat. Elizabeth and Jewel have questions.

"Ace, the restaurant health report has been posted." Elizabeth says.

"Yeah Ace, what's up with the negative report? There was a mention of moldy cheese."

He is embarrassed. He is so embarrassed about it, he doesn't have much to say.

"I'm working hard on replacing the head chef. He can't make a burger correctly. It is difficult to find good chefs in the area, but I'm looking."

"That sucks, Ace. I'm sorry you're dealing with an incompetent head chef."

"Thank you guys."

The burgers can be a hit or miss. One day, before Jewel was informed by Elizabeth of the health report, she ordered a medium well burger. When she returned to her dinner station to begin eating, the cow was still alive. Jewel had to head back to the Garden of Eden and ask that the burger be cooked medium.

"This is the chef's version of a medium burger," the waitress replied. Jewel was confused. From then on, she brought her own dinner to work in the evening.

Management

K aren is the boss lady aka the General Manager. Karen is a 5 ft. 5 inch, forty-three year old, 175 lb., blonde, White German American woman. She's married with four school aged children. Three of her children live at home and her eldest child is off at boarding school.

Jewel has arrived at work and Karen is behind the front desk counter working with Mary. Jewel speaks to everyone. Everyone speaks back to her but Karen.

Jewel logs into her computer station. Karen walks over flipping her hair with one hand on her hip.

"Jewel, can you work an extra shift this week? Mary asked for a day off."

"Yes, of course Karen. When would you like me to work?"

"Tomorrow! I know you had the day off, but this would be helpful."

"Okay, no problem."

"Thank you, Jewel," Mary says.

"You guys are welcome."

Karen turns to head out the front desk station area and says, "I'm leaving for the day." She walks towards her office to gather her things and heads to the door to leave.

"With all the money in the world that Karen has, she seems unhappy and insecure. Why is she always flipping her hair at me?" Jewel asks Mary.

"I don't know why she does that, maybe you're intimidating."

"Well, it sucks when rich people hate us poor people." Jewel flips her hair at Mary and puts both hands on her hips. "So what are you saying, I'm too strong, I'm too beautiful, I'm too independent, I'm too Black, I'm too real for Karen?"

"You got it!"

They both laugh in unison.

"I'm leaving now, Jewel," Mary says. "Thank you again for covering for me tomorrow. I have a doctor's appointment. I'm getting my first sonogram."

"No problem. How exciting!" Jewel squeals.

"I'm a little nervous and excited all at the same time." Mary lifted up her right arm to check the time on her Apple watch. "Thank you, Jewel. I have to run. I'm meeting my boyfriend for dinner."

"Okay good night and have fun."

Deenie Luckie

Mary quickly leaves the area and heads out.

Lucky for Jewel, she didn't have to spend too much time working with Karen. Karen was on shift one most of the time.

The first time Jewel noticed Karen showing her envious side was about two weeks after she was hired. She decided to swim in the hotel's pool before her shift. She swam for about an hour. When Jewel arrived at the front desk to start her shift; Karen approached her station, giving her the side eye. She commented how she herself is such a great swimmer. All while flipping her hair back and forth. Jewel realized at that moment; Karen had watched her on the camera. It creeped Jewel out so much that she decided to bike ride instead of swim before shifts. Karen would be nice some days. She'd tell Jewel how nice her outfit looked. Especially, when Jewel wore embossed Garden Tree Lakeside Resort employee's apparel.

Karen's energy/vibe was off; she's entitled. Her name suits her well. Jewel couldn't see herself spending any time with a person like Karen. She felt sad for her.

Karen's sidekick, Assistant General Manager Ginger whom she shares her office with is a sixty-one year old, 5 ft. 6 inches, blonde, White Irish American woman. Ginger has worked at the Garden Tree Lakeside Resort for twenty-eight years. A sneaky woman, don't turn your back on her.

One day, a Turkish family checked into the hotel. The family consisted of a husband, wife, and two very young children. Ginger spends time with the family. And then, there was only Ginger and Deniz, the husband. Ginger and Deniz have an affair within the six nights of the family's stay.

Housekeeping thought a guest's room was emptied. She went in the room and found Ginger in a doggy style sexual position with Deniz fucking her from behind. The housekeeper was shocked. She quickly ran out the room, slamming the door behind her.

The housekeeper was quickly walking past the front desk station and frowning.

Jewel stopped the housekeeper dead in her tracks.

"Hey what's wrong? Why are you looking sad and like you just saw a ghost?"

Whispering, she says, "I opened a room door and found Ginger having sex with a guest."

"No way, get out of here!"

"I'm serious. I just saw this." The housekeeper walks away holding her head down.

Elizabeth walks into the room and Jewel couldn't wait to tell her the gossip. "Elizabeth, the housekeeper just told me she opened a room's door and saw Ginger having sex with a guest."

"Oh yeah, the rumors have been flying around the hotel about it. It even reached Karen from what I heard. I have no idea if Karen has said anything to her or not. Ginger is still here, so I guess she's not fired. It's not my business so I don't want to have anything to do with that drama."

"I don't blame you. It's crazy for a manager to behave this way at work."

"Exactly!" Elizabeth acknowledges. The ladies continue along with their shift.

Months later…

Ginger vacationed in Turkey with Deniz and his family. She returned, in love. Ginger started planning her retirement in Turkey. House plans were created and blueprints were drawn. Lawyers are involved. Ginger's house that Deniz is building by hand is on his own land. She showed Jewel the blueprint and where her bedroom is located within the house.

Not to be judgmental, but Jewel is disgusted by this; she doesn't understand this lifestyle. Ginger is literally building her house on this woman's property so she can fuck her husband.

Ginger had no shame, she felt proud of her and Deniz's relationship. She told Jewel she wants to write a book on how he changed her life.

"I bet his wife can say the same. She can write a book on how this wealthy American woman felt comfortable enough with her husband to inject herself into their lives for an

eternity," Jewel thought.

When Ginger's at home in New York, she's sexing the Electrum telephone man. There's alway some kind of issue with the phones and the wi-fi. And since the account is so large, the same gentleman shows up each time. Ginger is responsible for showing the Electrum Company around the hotel. She spends quality time with him. Next thing you know, the rumors are flying around. She's sleeping with the phone man: dinner, dancing, laughing, dating, and fucking the damn married telephone man!

The Garden Tree Lakeside Resort is a family-owned business. Becky, Karen's niece, is the Human Resource Manager. Becky's a thirty-two year old, tall, blonde, White German American. She's a married woman with three school aged children. She can't be trusted. She steals and she's the person in charge of the payroll. Staff has to pay close attention to their hours worked.

Jewel knows this first hand. After having come in early to help out in laundry, she noticed the extra pay was not in her check. The next shift, she went to Becky for an explanation. Entering her office, Jewel notices the tall, slim woman typing (tap, tap) away at her computer. Her pale skin illuminated under the light coming from the screen. Her blue eyes shift to Jewel as she clears her throat in acknowledgement.

"I seem to be missing wages from my check," Jewel explains. "I worked 59 hours."

"You came in before your scheduled time," explains Becky.

"I was asked to come in early," says Jewel.

"So I owe you thirty minutes?"

"Yes, you do."

Innocent enough Jewel thought, but…

Then there was an issue with her sick pay. Jewel requested and received approved time off and just didn't get paid for it. At the time, she said nothing. There was no real reason behind her not following up. Either she forgot or she wasn't stressed about the money at the moment.

Next time…

Jewel's out and still she didn't receive her sick pay.

Again, she goes to confront Becky.

"Becky, where is my sick pay?"

Becky looks Jewel up and down with her blue eyes as if she's bothered.

"You'll have to get approval from your manager."

"Okay."

Jewel received an approval, but still no sick pay.

"Becky, I still didn't get my sick pay."

Becky makes a sigh sound as if Jewel was annoying her.

"Sorry about that, I'll take care of it on your next paycheck."

"Okay."

A couple weeks go by before Jewel sees the money. This is a repeat cycle that happens every time Jewel is out. Jewel is not often out, thank goodness.

Jewel's sick pay money is taxed more. Jewel is about done with this place. A few staff members are talking, their checks are being messed up, too.

A large number of staff members keep coming and going. Each person has complained that Becky messes up their paycheck.

Elizabeth and Jewel are working together one evening when Jewel asks her about it.

"Elizabeth, have you had any trouble with your paycheck being short? For example, when you're out sick."

"No, I email Becky and let her know when I'm out."

"Did you know some employees have complained about Becky shortening their paychecks?"

"Yes, I know. Court papers have been hand delivered to the front desk. For years, people have been suing them but I haven't had any issues. Becky knows what she is doing."

"Oh, so she steals from people on purpose?"

"Well, all I know is, Becky knows what she is doing."

Jewel agrees with Elizabeth. Becky knows exactly what she is doing. The scam has made the company thousands, upon hundreds of thousands of dollars.

Brenda was very hip to the scam. She, too, would confront Becky often. Becky was, therefore, trying other ways to get Brenda's money. Becky started taking Brenda's lunch time from her check. After Brenda realized what was going on, she started looking for new employment.

The other family members that helped Karen run the hotel include: Chad, Karen's brother; he's Head Maintenance man. And then there's Adam, Karen's nephew, he's Head Assistant Maintenance man.

Chad is the oldest of Karen's siblings. He's quickly approaching retirement. Chad is training Adam to become Head of Maintenance. When there is no houseman on duty in the evening, which happens often, the front desk clerks call Adam to come help out. For example, if there's a plumbing problem or a code four. A code four is when there's an issue with the toilet.

Elizabeth has issues with Karen. Karen would pit shift one versus shift two against each other. Elizabeth emailed Karen and asked to run the front desk while her and Ginger traveled. Shift two noticed Karen was training Stella from shift one for that position.

Stella is a young twenty-three year old, 5 ft 6 inch tall and a 180 lb., white American weed smoking woman from Saratoga Springs, NY. She lives one village away from Lake Avid. A fifteen-minute commute to the hotel. She lives in an apartment with her boyfriend and their cat. A very talkative lady, she talks fast and a lot. Jewel wonders if she's on cocaine because of how hyper she is.

Stella is the only front desk clerk who has a degree in hospitality. Karen may play favorites with Stella. Elizabeth surely thinks so. Karen has been training Stella to be the Head Supervisor of the Front Desk. The position that Elizabeth wants. Elizabeth has been working at the front desk three years longer than Stella.

Brenda and Jewel didn't care as much as Elizabeth about moving up the ladder. Brenda and Jewel were only interested in a hard day's work for a fair day's pay. They had no desire to become anyone's supervisor.

Karen wasn't interested in giving anyone on the second shift a chance. She spent most of her days working with shift one. Ginger spends most of her time with the second shift but only looks out for herself. She was not going to help Elizabeth become a supervisor.

Karen's favorite was Stella but Elizabeth is the person most familiar with Hotel Master. Elizabeth asked for a title change from Front Desk Clerk to Front Desk Supervisor. Explaining that she is the most advanced and skilled front desk clerk working at the Garden Tree Lakeside Resort.

Karen replied, "Let me speak with Ginger once she returns

from vacation."

Upon Ginger's return from her travels, Karen never approaches Elizabeth about the title change until...

"Jewel, please come here to my station. I want you to read this email I received from Karen."

She walks over to Elizabeth station. "What's going on?"

"Read this email please."

Elizabeth,

It never came to mind to train you for the front desk supervisor position. Stella is better qualified because she has a diploma in hospitality. I spend more time during the day with Stella, which makes it easier for me to train her. It would make no sense to train you for that position.

Karen

"I'm sorry to hear about this Elizabeth. So what are you going to do?"

"I'm not sure right now. I'm don't feel valued working here."

Elizabeth became so upset that she started looking for new employment. She finds new employment and is offered a few dollars more an hour.

A week later...

Elizabeth is walking around the hotel, up and down the stairs to the loft. She's snapping at everyone. When she finally makes her way back to her station, Jewel is interested to know what's going on with her.

"Elizabeth, what's going on with you today? You seemed to be in a bad mood."

"No, I'm not, I'm going to tell Karen about my new job offer today. I'm a little nervous. "

"Oh you'll be fine. Walk in her office and be confident."

"Okay, well I'm heading into her office now. Wish me luck."

"Good luck."

Elizabeth leaves the front desk area and walks toward Karen and Ginger's office. She's in the office for about ten minutes before she returns back to her station.

"Well, how did it go in there?" Jewel asked.

"I told her I was offered more money at the Mirror Lake Hotel. I asked her if she would match their offer and she said she couldn't."

"I'm sorry it didn't work out for you. So you told her that you're leaving?"

"No, she reminded me of my retirement money and now I'm second guessing if I should leave or not."

"Oh I see, I guess you have some thinking to do."

"I do."

Elizabeth and Jewel continue working, checking guests into the hotel.

Jewel enjoys working with Elizabeth and Brenda. It's always a different experience working with each lady. Brenda and Jewel have their sisterhood in common. Brenda is always laughing at the silliest thing anyone would say. Brenda stays positive but at the same time she refuses to let Karen and Becky belittle her.

There aren't many Black people around the community. Jewel gets excited just to spend time with her own race. Brenda isn't as excited to be with Jewel, just because she's Black, but because Jewel's cool people.

Jewel has a little crush on one of the coaches in the area. She feels comfortable speaking with Brenda about the drama involving the coach. Tanner, who is Brenda's long time boyfriend, is White. During their talks about the coach Brenda asked Jewel about his race.

"He's a Black man."

Brenda looks up with her eyes wide open.

"Why are you looking at me like that? I'm Black, too."

"I thought you would have been with a White man."

"Oh no, when I was younger, I would mess around with the White guys. At this point in my life I'm not really attracted to White men. They smell different than Black men. They age differently, too. The last time I was interested in a White man was about thirteen years ago. He was a model from Israel. We met in school. I couldn't keep my eyes off of him. He was so beautiful, but he had no interest in me at all."

"Well the coach is a jerk, he doesn't know what he is missing," says Brenda.

"I agree, there is less drama being single that's for sure."

Brenda is beautiful with soft brown coco skin tone. Jewel realizes Brenda doesn't see how beautiful she is as a Black woman. The small complaints she makes about herself makes Jewel question if Brenda would rather be a White woman. Brenda would say things about how overweight she is. How she doesn't wear her hair out in loose curls because she looks funny. That's the reason why she wears her hair up in a bun everyday. Jewel wants Brenda to have as much pride in herself as a Black woman as she does. She enjoys working with Brenda.

Brenda puts Jewel in mind of this lady, Jena. Jewel spent five years with Jena at the gym in NYC. Jena's of mixed race; light skinned, Black woman with green eyes. One day, Jena and Jewel were talking in the steam room. In the midst of all the steam, in the middle of their conversation, Jewel compared Jena's skin tone to a light skinned Black lady in the gym. The lady's Black, but was not of mixed race. Well, Jena chewed Jewel's head off and started screaming at her. "Don't compare me to a Black lady." Jewel was shocked. They had the same complexion. Jewel never looked at Jena the same. Jena wasn't proud of her Black heritage.

There are lots of Black women like Jena. White women are more entitled and privileged in the USA. Some Black women want to be included in that entitlement and have White privilege. Not just women either, men, too. Jewel immediately thought of Michael Jackson, for example. Michael Jackson cared more about being accepted in society. He wanted to be the most popular with the greatest amount of fame. He felt looking more White put him in a better position in the world. Unfortunately, Michael Jackson didn't look at the man in the mirror and see his natural beauty. With the power Michael Jackson had on the world, he could have helped little Black children with their own insecurities.

Jewel didn't think Brenda was that extreme. She hoped she wasn't. Jewel spent five years with Jena everyday at the gym and had no idea she had those feelings about herself. Jena was comfortable with Jewel because of them both being of mixed race. Society doesn't care about a person being of mixed race. A drop of Black blood and you're Black in this life. There are plenty of Black people who aren't proud. Those people don't know themselves. They don't look at themselves in the mirror but when they do, they don't like what they see.

While at work, Elizabeth and Jewel have a discussion on weight. Elizabeth refuses to eat vegetables and she watches Jewel drink vegetable juice every shift. She is always drinking juice, having dinner and she'll eat a cookie, too, yet she's a slim woman. Elizabeth doesn't eat as much as Jewel, yet, she complains how overweight she is.

Jewel keeps telling her to stop drinking soda and drink more water. And she did it, she stopped drinking the soda. But when she looked in the mirror the process wasn't moving fast enough. Change requires patience Jewel has learned.

Elizabeth has become a true friend. It was a small struggle, because Elizabeth doesn't have the greatest amount of patiences. Jewel lives a healthy lifestyle. Everyday, she makes herself a smoothie and a juice to carry along with her to work. Elizabeth living in a rural area, near the Amish people, has greatly benefited Jewel.

She brings her fresh fruits, vegetables, 100% grass-fed cow's milk yogurt from a creamery, tapped syrup from her husband's maple tree, and fresh honey from the bees. The best cut meats from her local butcher: chicken, lamb, bacon, and steaks. For a health conscious person like Jewel, this kind of food is heavenly.

The next day, time for work.

Clocked in at 3:00 p.m.

Brenda and Jewel are working this evening.

While laughing, Brenda calls the next in line forward. "May I help the next guest, please?"

The guest approaches her station and they can tell right away he is intoxicated. The smell from his clothes reaches Jewel's station; booze and cigarettes. While laughing, Brenda quickly does her usual check in spill. However, before the guest leaves he asks for directions to the Garden of Eden. He expressed that he is very hungry. Brenda points him in the right direction.

He walks away and Brenda and Jewel continue along with their shift. Thirty minutes later, the phone rings.

Jewel answers, "Hello, this is Garden Tree Lakeside Resort. How may I help you?"

"Jewel?"

"Yes, what's up Ace?"

"I just had to kick this drunk man out of the restaurant. He told me he checked into the hotel and is staying in room 207."

"Oh yeah, the drunk man Brenda checked in. What happened?"

"He walked into the restaurant past a family of four and grabbed one of their slices of pizza. And then he started to eat it in front of them!"

Jewel interrupts Ace, "Wow, that's not cool!"

Ace continues, "I had Tanner escort him back to his room. Tanner reported back. They walked past a kid that had a sandwich in his hand. The drunk guy turned to the kid and said, 'I am not touching your sandwich.' Then he touched the boy's sandwich and made a bell ringing noise. Tanner said when they got to the room, he noticed the guy had trashed it. All his clothes were in the shower with the water running. And the garbage can was flipped upside down in the toilet."

"That's crazy! Hopefully, the night will get better for you. Thank you for the update and I'll note his profile in Hotel Master. See you later?"

"Yes, I'll come and check on you and Brenda after I lock up."

"Okay, see you later."

They hang up. Jewel tells Brenda the latest drama. Jewel updates the man's profile in Hotel Master. She noted it in the shift report, as well.

The next day...

It's noontime, all expected rooms to check out have done so, except one. The intoxicated, pizza grabbing man front the previous night. Apparently he's passed out in his room. He didn't check out at 11:00 a.m. as expected. Ginger walks the hallway in the direction of the man's room. When Ginger gets to his room, with her right fist, she bangs on his room's door.

"Sir, it's check out time!" Ginger yells. With no response, Ginger heads back in the direction of front desk and calls his room in hopes of him answering the phone. With no answer, she calls the police.

Upon the police officer's arrival, Ginger and the officer head toward the problematic guest's room."

Bang! Bang!

"This is the police, open the door!" Still with no reply, the officer instructs Ginger, standing next to him, to unlock the door. She does as told.

Wham! The smell of puke slaps them in the face as the officer and Ginger enter the room.

"Smells like he had too much fun last night!" Ginger says in the moment of an awkward silence.

As they're looking into the room the officer says, "I'm going to have to agree with you, ma'am."

Due to the white lines of cocaine stacked up on the oakwood nightstand next to the bed, the police officer quickly wakes him up by grabbing his arm and yelling at him.

"Get up, you're under arrest for possession of narcotics. Let's go!" He's cuffed and taken out of the hotel, leaving all his belongings behind.

Let the Shenanigans Begin

I t's another day, time for work.

Clocked in: 3:00 p.m.

Check in begins.

A foreign family with a heavy accent is in Elizabeth's line to check in.

"May I help the next guest?" Elizabeth asks.

The guest approaches Elizabeth's station. "Yes, my family and I are here to check in."

Jewel is eavesdropping on Elizabeth's check in spill while doing her own.

Once the registration sheet is completed, she types (tap, tap) the details into Hotel Master. She notices that the guest's profile mentions there's a service dog accompanying the family. The guest requested a Speciality suite which is not a standard pet friendly room.

The pet fee is $100.00 per pet, an incentive guests have used to lie. The Deluxe Standard rooms, located on the third floor (same floor as the lobby), are the only pet friendly accommodations. This way the animals can exit the hotel quickly to relieve themselves.

Elizabeth decides to ask the two questions she's allowed under NYS law: *Is the animal required because of a disability; and what work or task has the animal been trained to perform (but may not ask that the animal demonstrate its ability to perform the work or task.)*

The guest appears to be confused by Elizabeth's questions, but he replies. "High blood pressure and barking."

She smiles. "Thank you for your answers."

She reminds the man that the dog is not to be left alone in the room. If there are any complaints of the dog barking or being left alone, he'll be charged the $100.00 pet fee.

Elizabeth completes her check in process.

The guest heads outside. Quickly, he returns with his barking dog, running around the lobby without a leash on. A pretty, fluffy, white, tall poodle, obviously excited to be out of the car.

"Sir, sir, your dog cannot be in the lobby without a leash on!" Elizabeth screams.

"Okay, okay, I'll put him on the leash now!"

The guest continues ranting with a heavy foreign accent. "Why are you giving me such a difficult time? The moment me and my family got here you have been rude to us. First, asking me questions about my dog and now yelling at me about my dog not being on a leash."

The lobby has a few people standing around who are minding their own business. People are standing around the large picturesque window overlooking Mirror Lake. Some are sitting on the sofa reading a book. A few are standing in line waiting to be checked in.

The lobby is now completely quiet at a standstill. Everyone has stopped what they're doing to listen to this man scream at Elizabeth.

"You're a racist, white, old lady! I'll be speaking with your manager."

There are no managers on duty at the time. Jewel raises her eyebrows at Elizabeth before taking a quick look around the room to see the faces of the guests standing in the lobby. Some of their faces look red and everyone is looking at Elizabeth with embarrassment while shaking their heads.

To calm things down, Elizabeth quickly speaks with the foreigner in a nice tone.

"Sir, did I tell you about the water show this evening at 7:00 p.m.? It will take place on the beach lawn," says Elizabeth.

He puts a smile on his face. "Yes, you did. My family and I are looking forward to the evening festivities."

"Okay then, enjoy your evening."

He and his leashed dog walk away.

Elizabeth showed such grace and class; Jewel is looking at her. She's impressed with how Elizabeth has handled herself. Elizabeth's mellow tone and the confidence she showed with her tall statue made Jewel proud. She wasn't bothered with the guest's rudeness because she knows who she is when it comes to racism. She didn't engage in his rude comments; instead, she put the fire out quickly by directing him to the evening events, the water show.

Jewel hoped Elizabeth wasn't a racist. Each day Elizabeth spent time working with Brenda and Jewel and she has never expressed any evil will due to racism. Jewel never heard Elizabeth say any racist comments or treat a guest of other races any differently than she treated her own race. Jewel didn't think she was. People of color have a fear of white people's hatred of them just because of the color of their skin. It's justified fear, proven throughout history and life.

Throughout the evening, this guest would come in and out of the lobby. Jewel would be standing right next to Elizabeth, chatting among themselves. They didn't discuss what just happened. It almost seemed silly to them. They both chalked it up to be just another entitled hotel guest.

It could be cultural differences which may be the cause of the confusion in the guest's head. Where he lives, dogs may not have the same restrictions as in America. However, if you're traveling to a foreign country with your dog, you may first want to inquire about their pet policies.

Jewel was shocked by how the guest accused Elizabeth of being racist because of her request to put the dog on the leash. Jewel doesn't want to believe people are racist unless they actually make a racist comment to her. She believes people are innocent until proven guilty. Until Elizabeth says a racist comment to her, she will continue to develop a friendship with her. To this day they never found out the family's race.

That night continued to move along smoothly... that was until 9:30 p.m.

The phone rings, Elizabeth takes the call. She hangs up and says, "I'll be back." She walks in the south direction of the hotel towards the rooms. A few minutes later, she returns to the front desk and tells Jewel what happened.

"You are not going to believe this."

Jewel's eyes widened with intense curiosity. "What happened this time?"

"A guest called and asked me to come to their room. There's blood on their sheets."

"No way!" Jewel screams.

There's no houseman on duty tonight. Only Elizabeth and Jewel are working the second shift. They're stuck with the houseman duties.

"Yes, I couldn't believe it. They said, after checking in earlier, they headed back out to meet up with their son. They are just now arriving in their room after being out all day and discovered the blood on the beds. You have to come help me. The blood is all over both of the beds. This is not right!" Elizabeth cries.

"Wow! Of course, I'll help you!"

"Please come down with me to laundry so we can get all new bedding."

"Okay."

Elizabeth posts a sign on the front desk counter, typed: *Stepped away, will return shortly.*

Both ladies walk in the south direction, down the hallway, towards the stairwell. They take the steps down to the first floor. Approaching the laundry room you walk through a set of gray double doors. Adjacent to the door entrance on your left, there are five large industrial washing machines and seven large industrial dryers. In the center of the room there are three large, 10x6 wood tables for folding linen. Ahead of the folding tables are walls of shelves. The shelves are stacked from floor to ceiling, lined with king and queen bed sheets, bed comforters, bath rugs, bath mats, shower curtains, pool towels, and more. When you walk into the laundry room on the right are the dirty laundry bins. The bins are stacked high with soiled linen.

They grabbed two sets of queen sheets, each set includes: two-flat sheets and a fitted sheet with four pillow cases. Housekeeping doesn't change the comforters on the beds in each room. After different guests have slept in the beds, the same comforter is placed back on the bed. It's a practice the ladies feel to be nasty, but it is what it is.

To be fair, hotels don't change pillows between each guest's stay either. The same pillow is used over and over, for months or even years at a time. At least the comforter is sandwiched in-between two sheets, just like the pillow is stuffed into a pillowcase. The extra folded blanket on the edge of the bed however, is not sandwiched into a sheet or any washed covering. It's used over and over until a noticeable stain or spot is on it. Just plain ole nasty!

Elizabeth and Jewel are fully aware that not changing the comforter is a normal practice. So, Elizabeth didn't even think to grab two queen comforters; Jewel had to remind her.

"Elizabeth, since you're standing next to the comforters, grab two of them. We have to change them. We can't let the guests know we don't change the comforters."

"Oh yeah, you're right, Jewel, especially with blood on the bed."

Elizabeth grabbed two comforters. They now have a bin full of sheets and comforters. They leave the laundry area and jump onto the elevator to the third floor. They exit the elevator walking towards the guest's room.

"Let me go check the front desk and make sure no one is waiting for assistance. The room is right here, you go get started stripping the beds and I'll be right back with you," says Elizabeth.

"Okay."

Jewel knocks on the door while putting on her gloves. The guest opens the door and Jewel introduces herself. Her husband is sitting on the chair at the table on his laptop. The television is on, a crime show is playing. Jewel's favorite kind of television show. She speaks to the husband. The usual, "Hi Sir, how are you doing?" And then Jewel sees it, the blood! Jewel goes into shock. Her mind is having difficulty processing what she is seeing. She's having a few seconds of a full blown out, unreal, surreal, she can't believe what she is seeing, kind of moment. Jewel begins to strip the beds. She apologizes to the guests for this horrible injustice of having the bad luck of getting this room. Even though Jewel is fully aware this is not her fault; she feels really bad.

The guests were calm, nice, and they didn't seem mad. Jewel is surprised at how relaxed they are. While Jewel is removing the sheets from the bed, her and the wife engage in small talk. They talked about what was on television.

"Oh yes, you have the TV station on the ID channel. That's my favorite channel to watch. I love figuring out who the killer is. I should have been a detective," says Jewel.

"Yes, this is my husband and I favorite channel, too. We watch the ID channel almost everyday.

"Sometimes, I feel bad that I enjoy the channel so much, because a lot of these stories are true. People are killed and I enjoy watching because of my twisted sense of entertainment," Jewel expressed.

The wife giggles at Jewel, and says. "I understand what you mean, but we didn't kill them."

"You have a good point," says Jewel.

The wife and Jewel share a small giggle together.

Her husband didn't have anything to say. He had a very serious look on his face. He was sitting in the chair, at the desk, typing away on his laptop. He would repeatedly look up at the television and then back to typing (tap, tap, tap...)

Jewel understands how finding the blood on the sheets would be upsetting. Jewel is upset; she hopes someone is fired! However, to keep the peace and calm in the room, Jewel continues working and doesn't mention the reason she's in the room in the first place.

The wife did make a point to let Jewel know they paid a lot of money for the room. And that they had expected better accommodations.

"My dog would expect better accommodations than this," Jewel thought. Jewel doesn't even have a dog. The wife made a point to let her know they were from Long Island and are here visiting their son at the local boarding school, North Mountain Academy.

Elizabeth returns and they quickly work together to get both beds made. They let the guest know that they'll be speaking with management about the situation. In the meantime, they compensated them with breakfast vouchers to be redeemed at the Garden of Eden. They were thankful and expressed they knew this wasn't their job to make beds.

Elizabeth and Jewel head back to the front desk. Their shift is wrapping up for the evening. Ronnie has arrived for his shift. Ronnie is the night auditor. Ronnie's position includes but is not limited to prepare the registration sheets and attach the parking pass for the morning shift.

The third shift hours are 11:00 p.m.-7:00 a.m. worked by Ronnie aka "Killer." He's thirty-one years old, 5 ft. 10 inches, 220 lb. overweight man with the Santa Claus stomach. He has a long beard. He's bald on the top of his head with short black hair in the back. He wears a black tee shirt with black jeans everyday. Ronnie's a White American weed smoker, who's anti-social. There's a reason for Ronnie's nickname "Killer." He doesn't listen to music or watch television. He likes to play video games. He's a no nonsense type of character.

Most people really have no idea what he looks like. He wears a mask everyday. Brenda and Jewel have seen his face once, maybe twice. Elizabeth worked with him before the CoronaVirus. She knows how he looks. The staff isn't sure if it's because he works in the middle of the night for him being so "different."

Before each outgoing shift leaves for the day/night, they're required to pass off the day's drama. In addition to verbal communication, each shift has to create a shift report at the end of their shift. The shift report is emailed to all front desk staff and Management.

Ronnie's reports are so funny. He says the least, most nights his report read:

A quiet night.

Or if Ronnie's in a mood, this is an example of a detailed report from him:

? Maybe we need to double the houseman salary to keep them around longer than a month...

? Lots of no shows.

? Folio 217855 has more than a thousand transactions on it and should be cleared.

? The entire fourth floor, south, and seemingly the second floor, are all having trouble with TV/internet services.

? 123 can't control their heat.

? 333 reported being unable to use their television properly.

? 400 has called down half a dozen times tonight to complain and ask about managers, so, get ready.

For some reason he just decided to put question marks in front of each statement. Funny.

Ronnie and Jewel share the same computer station. He speaks to both Elizabeth and Jewel with his nonchalant attitude. As Elizabeth and Jewel are standing around, updating him on the day's drama, Ronnie grabs the telephone and yells. "What's all over this phone? It's oily!"

Jewel replies, "Oh that's the coconut oil from my hair."

"Well, can you at least clean it off?"

"It's not going to kill you. I'll wipe it clean next time."

The other staff members getting ready to clock out with Elizabeth and Jewel are standing in the back room, just snickering and laughing.

"Ronnie is an ass," Jewel says, snickering with them. Elizabeth and Jewel walk out together.

Summer

The Garden of Flower

T he Garden of Flower Spa is operated by Shannon. The spa offers hair care, facials, massages, manicures, pedicures, and aromatherapy services.

Jewel has visited the Garden of Flower in the past. She likes a good facial once in a while. She can go a couple years without cutting her hair. It's almost been three years since Jewel's last hair cut.

The reason it has been so long is because Lake Avid is a predominantly White community. Jewel feels uncomfortable with White people cutting her hair and to be fair she pretty much feels the same about a Black person dealing with her hair, too.

Jewel's of mixed race [African American, Native American, and Caucasian] so her hair is very curly, thick, coarse, and soft all at the same time. She's comfortable with the Spanish or mixed race people cutting her hair due to the similarity in their hair type.

However, there are no Spanish, mixed raced hairdressers around the community. Jewel has a birthday coming up and she's heading to Jamaica this time. She schedules a haircut at the spa and it is long overdue.

Shannon was Jewel's first next door neighbor when she

moved to Lake Avid and she's a weed dealer, too. So, Jewel and Shannon have established a relationship. They don't hang out together out here in these streets, but they do have their moments of girl talk.

First appointment; Shannon didn't show up. Upon Jewel's arrival to the spa the receptionist informed her; Shannon's been depressed. Shannon texts Jewel. "Sorry, I'll make it up to you" and she doesn't have to pay for the next appointment. Jewel wondered if Shannon was nervous about cutting her hair. She knew Shannon had not much or if any experience cutting ethnic hair.

The date of her next appointment arrives. Shannon sets Jewel up in the chair and drapes her with a waterproof cloth. She starts touching Jewel's hair and talking.

"I don't get to do Black people's hair often. They're just no ethnic people around here. When a Black woman comes into the shop, she usually sits in my chair with a wig on. When I go to take off the wig it smells so bad. I feel like throwing up! I have to use disposal combs for their hair."

While Shannon is talking, Jewel observes her through the mirror, their differences on full display. But Jewel was a tiny bit impressed, Shannon could at least say "Black people." People in the community act like saying "Black people" is a taboo.

Although they are around the same age, Shannon is an average height, overweight White woman. Jewel's recreational relationship with Shannon was probably the only thing they had in common.

"Oh my, and when they ask me to blow dry their hair! I don't have time to blow dry their hair."

Jewel doesn't say anything, she's just listening. *"Oh boy, this is a hair salon,"* she thought. *"Blow drying the hair should be part of the time spent doing the hair, if it's requested."*

Shannon keeps talking.

"You know what, you have hair just like my mother."

"Really?"

Jewel has heard this one plenty of times. People will tell her, their best friend, cousin, mother, brother, sister, baby mama, all have hair like Jewel. But, really it's a weave. At the end of the day, if you're not of mixed or Spanish race, most likely your best friend, mother, brother, cousin, baby mama does not have Jewel's hair type.

Shannon continues, on and on, that her mother spends forty minutes a day blow drying all of her curls out.

Jewel can't imagine taking that much time out of her day to blow dry her hair. She doesn't have that kind of patience. She would rather sleep.

Jewel has the kind of hair the Black community calls "good hair" and what the White community calls "Black people's hair." White people look at color first and just assume all Black people have the same hair type. For example, Elizabeth and Jewel were talking about hair the other day at work. Jewel mentioned she was finally getting her wild hair cut.

"My Jamaican girlfriend has hair like yours," Elizabeth said. "She goes to the salon about every six weeks to get that stuff put in her hair." She never refers to her best friend by name, always her Jamaican Girlfriend.

Elizabeth has very thin, short, blonde hair. Jewel is sure Elizabeth's confused. She is not educated on the matter of Black people's hair types.

"You mean a perm?" Jewel asked.

"Yes."

Jewel has never had a perm. She knew for sure Elizabeth's Jamaican girlfriend doesn't have her hair type.

"Elizabeth, I have been to Jamaica a few times and I don't recall seeing too many, if any, Jamaicans with my hair type."

Shannon looks at Jewel for a moment before she continues on..."You take very good care of your hair, it's a little dry, but not much."

"Okay," Jewel replies.

Then she continues to explain each cut.

"I'm pulling it a little bit and I'm cutting it at an angle."

When she scheduled her appointment, she asked to have her hair cut in layers. Jewel thought Shannon was doing a good job. Not a great job like the Spanish, but she was satisfied with the end results. The conversation was weird but her heart was not in a racist direction. People are not educated on the issues of race and ethnic hair. Shannon was telling Jewel her personal experience of doing a Black women's hair. Not being educated on race doesn't necessarily make you a racist. The times Jewel has spent talking with Shannon never once had a tone of racism. She was so involved in doing drugs, racism appeared to be the last thing on her mind.

Their phone conversations include talk about the asshole man that is not worth a dime of her time.

"He's always cheating on me. He just moved this tramp of a piece of trash in his house across the street! He even called himself trying to hide it from me. Showing up in the middle of the night with a Uhaul truck like I wasn't going to figure it out. I heard them moving in and out! I can see them out of my window for fuck sake." Shannon screams! "And everytime he leaves his house in that Ford F150 it makes a loud rumbling noise. Its like torture to me."

"Shannon move, don't continue putting yourself through this drama. I'm so sorry you're going through this shit. He's not worth it." Jewel adds her two cents to the conversation.

When they're on the phone, Jewel believes Shannon is very high. Her voice is slurred and fuzzy while talking. Jewel felt sad for Shannon. She knew Shannon had cocaine and heroin addiction. Jewel watched Shannon inject heroin while at her house one day.

The next day after her appointment, Jewel is looking good with her haircut and feeling good, anticipating her birthday trip to Jamaica.

Upon arrival to work she has an extra boost of energy in her steps. Jewel approaches her work station with all smiles. She speaks to the first shift before they head out.

"Good afternoon, everyone."

"Hi, Jewel."

"What's going on with you today, Jewel? You're looking all happy with your cute purple dress on. Do you have a date tonight?" Stella asked while gathering her things to leave for the evening.

"Ha ha that's funny, if only my prince would walk through that door. No, I just got my haircut and I'm looking forward to my vacation. Do you have anything exciting going on tonight?" Jewel asks Stella.

"No, same crap as usual. Well, have a good evening. I'll see you tomorrow, if you're working."

"Okay, good night."

Stella walks away.

Clocked in: 3:00 p.m.

At 3:05 p.m., Jewel's at the front desk and she calls for the next guest.

"Hello, may I help the next person in line?"

"Yes, may I check in? I know I am an hour early, but I thought I should ask to see if the room is available. I'm from Long Island and it was a six-hour drive to get here."

"Yes, sir. Let me check for you. What's your last name?"

"It's Avihu Jerafi, from Long Island."

Jewel checks Hotel Master to see if the room is available and it is.

"Mr. Jerafi, your room is ready. Let's get you and your family settled in. I see you will be staying in our Big Slide Suite. Those accommodations should be a very nice fit for you and your family."

"Yes, they are, thank you. I'll need a good night's rest after that long drive from Long Island."

"Mr. Jerafi, I understand. I spent parts of my childhood growing up in Long Island. My daughter was born in Rockville Centre in Mercy Hospital."

Mr. Jerafi eyes POPPED out of his socket!

"You?"

"Yes, me!"

People from Long Island come into the hotel and they want to announce to everyone that they come in contact with that they're from Long Island. Long Islanders are probably the most rich, entitled, racist people in the world. Jewel knows from experience; she spent some of her childhood growing up in West Hempstead, Long Island.

Out of her mother's five children, the three oldest were born in Queens, NY. The two youngest siblings were born in Mercy hospital in Rockville Centre. Mercy Hospital is the same hospital Jewel's daughter, Jolly, was born. In addition, Jewel's grandmother died in Mercy hospital. She has a strong connection to Long Island.

Jewel recalls being called a nigger growing up on the Island by the White children. In the 80s, before her family moved to West Hempstead, the White families in the community had a petition going around to try and stop Black families from moving into "their" neighborhood.

Jewel would ask herself, "*Why?*" Why are the White people trying to keep the Black families out of the neighborhood? An interesting and sad question for a young girl to ask herself. "*It should be the other way around,*" Jewel thought. "*Who would want the Whites living in their neighborhood?*"

History has proven the real killers in the world are White! White serial killers and White rapists are larger in numbers than within the Black race. It's all about the money. White people have the money in America. Black people bring down the property value. CAPITALISM at its finest!

Ha! Jewel thought the real reason behind Black families'
denial in the White communities is because White men are
mad. The White men are mad because Black men are
known to be better lovers with bigger dicks. Society will
see a White woman with a Black man more often than
you'll see a Black woman with a White man. FACTS!

There is no other race that can understand a Black man
better than a Black woman. Even while the Black man is
married to a White woman. The White wife will always be
missing an understanding within her Black husband. It's
because of the culture and soul of the Black American race.

Black people's blood lines carry the secret to the fountain
of youth. It's a White woman's dream to grow old and
wrinkle free with the same beauty and grace as a Black
woman. Tanning just isn't making the cut these days.
White women keep those plastic surgeons in business.

Plastic surgeons love themselves some White women.
Perfect example; the Kardashians. Jewel's not mad at these
ladies for having billionaire Black babies. The Karadasians
are living a life most White women dream about. Fucking
Black men with a big dick, producing mixed billionaire
babies!

Jewel has had some fond childhood memories growing up
on Long Island. She's not painting a picture of it being all
bad. Jewel and her family were different. There were a
handful of Black families living in the neighborhood.
Black people have swag. Black people will always look

and be different when set up in a White community.

Long Islanders conveniently forget there are full blown
Black communities on Long Island. When Jewel was
growing up, for example, Lakeview, Hempstead (the place
Eddie Murphy lived), and Malvern, just to name a few.
White people who live on the Island know there are Black
communities on Long Island. They'd rather act stupid.

Mr. Jerafi is standing in this hotel, at Jewel's front desk
station looking at her as if he's never seen a Black person
before. Let alone a whole community of Black families on
Long Island.

Working at the front desk taught Jewel that people from
Long Island still have the same attitudes of entitlement
today in 2023 as they did back in 1980. Yes, Jewel knows
Long Island is one of the richest places to live in the world,
but who cares, but them.

Mr. Jerafi continues.

"Really? Where are you from? Off the Long Island
Expressway?"

"No, the Southern State Parkway, Eagle Avenue exit."

"Oh, Nassau County?"

"Yes, that's correct."

Another thing people from Suffolk County think is they
naturally have more money than people from Nassau

County. They tend to stick their noses up people's asses a little less. However, Nassau County, Long Island, is one of the wealthiest counties in America, more so than Suffolk County. Suffolk County has the Hamptons, a playground for the rich and famous.

"Here comes Mr. Jerafi's wife." Jewel assumed. She's approaching the counter and stands right next to him.

Jewel speaks, "Hi."

Mr. Jerafi introduces her.

"This is my wife, Mrs. Jerafi."

"Hi, Mrs. Jerafi. How are you doing today?"

"A little tired from our drive. Thank you. Did my husband tell you we drove in from Long Island?"

"Yes, he did."

"Honey, come to find out she has spent lots of her childhood growing up on Long Island and her daughter was born on the Island, too."

"Really?!?! May we have extra towels delivered to our room everyday? We would also like our bed sheets changed and made EVERYDAY."

"Yes," exclaims Jewel.

"Really? Everyday?" Jewel internally screams. But of

course she keeps quiet, documents Hotel Master, and sends a red flag out to housekeeping.

She completes the check in spill and sends the Jerafis' on their way.

Dirty Laundry

Jewel is gleaming from ear to ear showing all her teeth. After the J1 stays for the season, there is always a big employee shortage. Karen emails the staff to pitch in extra hours. This is the one time of the year when all the full-time staff can make overtime. She's always excited about overtime. The extra hours can be spent in the laundry or housekeeping department.

J1s are foreign college students from undeveloped countries who travel to the USA on a student work visa. The hotel provides housing to them on a weekly basis for $110.00. In NYC, the city has a large number of foreigners, especially illegal Mexicans. So, this will be Jewel's first experience interacting with J1s working at the resort.

The J1s perform the jobs that lots of Americans feel are beneath them, like cleaning toilets. In NYC, the Mexicans are doing those jobs. There are no Mexicans living in Lake Avid. So, there are staff shortages throughout the community.

Laundry is Jewel's favorite department to pick up some extra shifts. Jewel tells Karen right away. That way, she will schedule her before anyone else. Chandler and Jack are the laundry attendants. They work 11:00 a.m. to 7:00 p.m. Jewel will be working with them.

Chandler has been the laundry attendant with the Garden Tree Lakeside Resort for twenty-eight years. Chandler is a fifty-four year old, 5 ft. 1-inch tall, gay, male who is half French Canadian and half Native American, from the Mohawk tribe. He speaks English, French, and Kanien'keha. Chandler is a sad, lonely, man, who seems to never be happy with life.

He has a live-in boyfriend, Dakota. Dakota is an alcoholic and a recovering meth addict that Chandler met at the hotel. It's an obvious relationship of convenience, no love.

Jewel is helping the guys out in laundry today. She and Chandler arrive at the same time. Chandler is being his usual snappy self. To liven his mood, Jewel takes the bait.

"Chandler, what's going on with you today?"

He walks slowly through the laundry making his way to the radio. He turns on the music. Beyonce's Single Ladies is playing. Great, just what Jewel wants to listen to- a song about being single.

"Dakota is in the hospital. He has been in pain and the doctors are doing tests and blood work to figure out what's wrong with him."

Chandler continues walking slowly with his head down towards the bins full of dirty laundry. He puts on latex gloves and begins loading the washing machines.

Jewel is grabbing towels and folding them out of the bin leftover from the previous evening.

"Oh no, Chandler, I'm sorry to hear that. I'm sure he'll be okay."

"I hope so. You know he was heavy into drugs and he used needles. He's not doing that anymore but he still drinks a lot."

"Everything will be okay. Try not to worry too much about it. I know it's easier said than done."

Jack shows up, late, but he's here.

"Good morning," Jack says. "How is everyone?"

"We're okay, Jack. How are you today?" Jewel replies.

Jack is smiling from ear to ear. He loves when Jewel works in the laundry department.

"I'm great! It's nice that you're working with us today."

Jewel likes to sing whatever is on the radio. She'll have both of them smiling at some point in the day. And she works hard which makes life much easier for the department.

Chandler has all the washing machines going. He starts to fold sheets quietly while they listen to the radio.

When Jewel is working in the laundry department, she gets to hear all about Dakota's drunken nights and how Chandler has to take care of him. When Jewel asks why he deals with Dakota's behavior, he says it's better than being alone.

Chandler has a dog and a cat. He talks about how they make him happy. He likes to cook. Chandler and Jewel have that much in common. They go over recipes and discuss what they'll cook for dinner. He would tell stories of walking his dog and playing with his cat. So, Chandler did have a tiny bit of joy in his life.

In addition to all Chandler's troubles at home. He's never happy at work. The laundry department is always short-handed. The bins are always piled high with dirty linens. Chandler and Jack are always crying and trying to play catch up to make sure there are enough linens for housekeeping in the morning. Jack is always snapping about something, too. Jewel usually has no idea what about.

Jack is a 5 ft. 8 inch, forty-one year old, white American male with Aspergers. He lives in a group home with others diagnosed with mental health. Jack and Jewel have something in common. He likes to bike ride like she does. They bike ride together before his scheduled shift begins. In the beginning, the riding was okay. After a week, it became too much for Jewel. Jack started to become obsessed with biking with Jewel.

First, he didn't show up on time for their scheduled bike ride. He would look for Jewel during working hours to bike ride. And then, he started keeping up with Jewel's work schedule. He knew what time she was at work and her days off. He would call during work hours about biking. It annoyed Jewel. She didn't want to hurt his feelings, but at the same time she just wanted to enjoy her bike rides without the drama.

At moments, Jewel did enjoy the little bit of company. But, she didn't want it to feel like a chore. Jack was stealing the joy of her morning bike rides.

Ginger becomes aware of the bike riding drama.

"Jewel, if you like, I'll put a call into his health aid. They'll speak with him," Ginger offered.

"No, that's not necessary to call anyone. The season is almost over, I'll deal with it until then."

The front desk staff members started joking around with Jewel, saying things like Jack was her boyfriend.

Brenda was the funniest of them all, asking Jewel, "Where are you and Jack having dinner for the evening? Tanner and I want to have a double date."

She would even say things like, "So did you hook up with Jack last night?"

Jewel would reply, "Now Brenda, that's disrespectful and nasty."

Brenda is always smiling and laughing while joking around with Jewel.

Here goes Elizabeth putting her two cents in.

"Well Jewel, you do need a man." Elizabeth just isn't laughing when she makes her comment. She is serious and Jewel knows this because Elizabeth is looking her in the eyes with no smile on her face.

Elizabeth knows good and well Jewel is not attracted to Jack. Since Jewel is the single one, there's always a comment about her getting a man, especially from Elizabeth.

Jewel looks at Elizabeth as if she's confused. "Elizabeth, not everyone needs a man to be happy. But, you're right, a little dick once in a while would be nice."

"See that's what I'm talking about, Jewel. You need a man!"

"Well enough of this talk of me needing a man. I'll be okay."

"If you say so."

Jack has a girlfriend, Liz. They live together at the group home. Jewel met Liz once. Jewel ran into her and Jack on the street. Jack introduced Jewel as his co-worker and as the person he rides with in the morning. After meeting Liz, she starts to get involved with telling Jack he can't ride with Jewel on some days. Making up weird excuses. For example, the weather would become an excuse. It's either too cold or too hot outside, but it's 60 degrees out.

Dakota, Chandler's boyfriend, has become very sick, his liver is failing and he is admitted into the ICU. Surgery is completed. He's put on a strict diet and rehab to recover. Chandler is so stressed. Not because of being sad for Dakota, he's stressed because of how this is an inconvenience to his life.

Chandler is walking slowly up to the front desk with his head held down as usual. He approaches Elizabeth and Jewel and they inquire about Dakota and how he is doing.

Chandler starts crying, "What about me? Why doesn't anyone care about what I'm dealing with?"

"How are you doing, Chandler?" Elizabeth asks.

"I've had better days. I'm all alone."

"Well, you have your animals," Jewel says.

That remark put a smile on Chandler's face for a moment. "Yes, I do have them."

"Things will get better for you Chandler. You'll see," Elizabeth says

Elizabeth and Jewel just looked at each other and him.

"Thank you guys for listening to me. I appreciate it."

"You're welcome, Chandler," Elizabeth says.

Both the ladies say, "Good night, Chandler."

"Feel better, okay." Jewel comments as Chandler walks away.

Jewel thinks, "*Dude you have your health.*"

According to Chandler, he doesn't go visit Dakota in the hospital. He keeps the front desk clerks abreast to all that is happening. Dakota asked Chandler to bring him his laptop. Chandler refused and told Dakota he had to rest and recover and not be on his laptop. Elizabeth and Jewel are confused. Why is Chandler holding back the man's laptop and not going to see him?

Nightly, Chandler comes to the front desk complaining that he has to pay all the bills and how he is alone. Dakota's illness has become all about what Chandler wants. Dakota was making his life uncomfortable by being in the hospital. Chandler noticed Dakota's on Facebook. He'd leave messages onto people's sites, but he wasn't returning Chandler's call.

Of course, Chandler comes to the front desk to ask for help to make sense of all this drama he has going on with Dakota.

Jewel is the only person at the front desk counter available to listen and so she does.

"Jewel, why do you think Dakota is avoiding me? He hasn't been returning my calls."

"I'm sorry Chandler, I have no idea. Have you gone to the hospital to see him?"

"No, I have been so busy and the hospital is over an hour away from my house."

"Oh, well maybe he is waiting for you to visit him to talk, but I don't know, Chandler. Can you go visit him on your day off?"

"I'll try, but those are the days I'm running around getting my errands done."

"Well, that's probably the best way to get all your questions answered."

"You're right, Jewel. Thank you for the chat!"

"You're welcome."

Chandler slowly walks away with a grin on his face.

Dakota is finally released from the hospital and Chandler's not happy. He has to take care of a sick man with no monetary help. Dakota's condition gets worse while at home with Chandler. He's readmitted back to the local hospital. At the hospital, his condition doesn't improve. He is eventually transported to the city hospital and is informed that he has to start liver dialysis to get better. Dakota is in full blown depression and isn't feeling loved by anyone, especially Chandler.

It's another day...

Chandler and Jewel are working in the laundry together. Chandler receives a call on his cell phone. He approaches Jewel with a grin on his face, looking happy, which is unusual.

"That was Dakota's sister. She told me Dakota has passed away."

"WOW! I'm so sorry, Chandler!"

Jewel thought, "*I bet you'll think twice before you decide to let another drug addict move into your house because of loneliness.*"

"It's okay, he's in a better place now."

"I didn't see that coming," says Jewel.

"He gave up! He also had Hepatitis C."

"Oh, WOW!"

"*I hope he wasn't dry boning you in the ass.*" was Jewel's first thought.

Of course, that doesn't come out of her mouth. The second thing she thinks is, "*How in the world does a man in his 40's living in New York State get Hepatitis C?*" By law, New Yorkers have to get a Hep C vaccine to enter into the public school system. Being from NYC, she's also aware of the loopholes.

For example, in March 2016, the Orthodox Jewish community in Williamsburg, Brooklyn, had a chicken pox outbreak. Over 75 children in Williamsburg, Brooklyn, had the chicken pox and all within several months of one another. The Jewish community uses religion to back up not vaccinating their children.

Dakota was Native American from the Mohawk Tribe. The tribe may have their own laws as well.

"How did he get hepatitis C?"

"From sharing needles during his drug use days."

"Oh, such a sad story, I'm sorry to hear that."

Chandler looks at Jewel and smiles. They quietly continue working while listening to music. She continues folding towels and Chandler folds sheets.

At that moment, it was as if Chandler magically found peace and some kind of freedom in his life. It was difficult for Jewel to understand his emotions, especially in the moment.

The shift wraps up and Jewel heads home. This is overtime, so Jewel has to make sure she's sleeping and eating correctly. When she arrives home, Jewel still has Dakota's death on her mind. She decides to google Hep C. Come to find out, there is no vaccine for it.

Housekeeping

B renda isn't that the guy who beats up that lady in housekeeping pulling up in front of the hotel?" Jewel observed and asked.

Brenda is looking out the window checking the car out.

"Oh yes, that's him. I hope he doesn't come in here messing with her."

"We should be prepared for anything."

"Yeah, you're right."

The double doors open and the housekeeper's boyfriend strolls in. He approaches Brenda's station.

"Hi, if you don't mind, can you please tell Amanda that her man is here?"

"Yes, no problem."

Brenda grabs the radio and dispatches Amanda to the front desk.

Amanda arrives at the front desk. Her and the boyfriend are having small talk. Brenda and Jewel can't hear anything, but she is twitching and pointing her finger at him. The next thing we know, he grabs Amanda's arm. She starts to pull her arm away from him and screams, "Let me go!"

Brenda and Jewel are staring at each other.

Jewel comments, "Here we go with the drama."

Brenda yells at them, "We can't have this yelling in the lobby!"

"Everything is okay, he was just leaving," Amanda says.

"I'll be back," says the boyfriend.

"Brenda, I think he's one of those zombie people on that meth," Jewel brings to Brenda attention.

When she owned a health food store, Jewel didn't get to see too many people walk into the shop with drug issues. She wasn't aware that there was a Crystal Methamphetamine (Meth) problem in the community until she started working at the Garden Tree Lakeside Resort.

You can usually tell these people by their rotten teeth and zombie-like exterior. Several people in housekeeping have missing teeth and look tired and run down.

"I think both of them are using meth. She looks crazy, too," Brenda replies.

"Yeah, you have a point."

Meth addicts were in the housekeeping and housemen department. The turnaround in these departments was weekly to monthly for one reason or another. Staff members realized Karen was a drama queen and didn't want to deal with it. People also realized Becky was shortening their paychecks.

Housekeeping is the department that has all the 411 on the hotel. If you want to know who is sleeping with whom or where to get the drugs from just ask someone in the housekeeping department.

The Head of Housekeeping, Ellen, has been working for the Garden Tree Lakeside Resort for seventeen years. Ellen is a fifty-five year old, 185 lb. white American woman. She lives with and takes care of her elderly mother. She has three adult sons who live in other states. At any given time, Ellen has between ten to sixteen housekeepers working under her.

The housekeeping department was Jewel's least favorite department to work in for overtime. However, there is a big issue with the front desk staff working in the housekeeping department. Housekeepers are paid $2.00 more per hour than the front desk staff. They also receive $5.00/per day, per room, plus any tips left behind in the rooms.

When Brenda found out about housekeepers making more money, she made a big stink about doing the same job for less. It worked. But every time Jewel worked in the laundry or housekeeping, it was for time and half. Jewel worked in those departments for overtime pay only.

When the hotel is closed in the off season, Karen has to make up front desk hours in other departments. So there would be times the front desk staff would help out and not make the time and half. And this was Brenda's biggest concern.

Two weeks later, Brenda and Jewel received an extra $250.00 on their paychecks. Elizabeth didn't have interest in housekeeping or the laundry department. She would help decorate the lobby during the holidays to make extra cash.

The extra $250.00 in Jewel's check made her think. *"If Brenda never made a stink about the money, would Karen have given it to us?"* Jewel felt used and abused!

Ellen teamed up the front desk staff with a housekeeper. Together, they worked to clean the rooms. Sometimes, not all, but some of the housekeepers would open up all their room doors, collect all tips, and not share.

The hotel rooms are your standard nasty rooms. They had to be vacuumed or swept. Beds striped and made. Bathroom cleaned and window/mirrors wiped, as well. They could find an exploded can of soda in the freezer or a used condom in-between the sheets. Housekeepers have a nasty job dealing with bodily fluids. Someone has to do it, and it should be done with pride.

The housekeeping department is always full of drama. For example, in the hotel, a male housekeeper, a houseman, and a male beautician are all in a sexual relationship.

"Elizabeth, have your heard the latest drama going around about, Joe, Brian, and Mike fucking each other at the same time?"

"Yes, you know I have. Joe has seen me in the hallway crying that Brian and Mike go behind his back sometime and have sex without him. The drama and gossip that goes on around the hotel about the three men is funny!"

"I know, I think it's hilarious, too. Mike is too young for them to be fooling around with him. I believe he's 18 years old," Jewel says.

"Well, he's an adult. The gossip is that Mike has other partners whom he has sex with. At 18 years old I'm sure he has a hard time controlling that beast in his pants. Do you see how big his shoes are?"

"That's so nasty. That's how people get HIV. I agree he does have some big feet. Big feet equal big penis is what the word on the street is."

Both ladies are laughing!

"I know, you're right Jewel!"

Brian, the housekeeper in the threesome is also the hotel's weed dealer. He has all the potheads running around looking for him to buy their weed. Jewel has no idea where the people with the rotten teeth get their drugs from. She never cared to ask.

Another conflict between housekeeping and the front desk staff. Elizabeth and Jewel are the main upgrade front desk clerks. Of course with Elizabeth being the Queen. Rules are set forth that must be followed to receive an upgrade.

Ellen's upset that Jewel had an upgrade in the middle of a two-night stay. Her department has to do all the cleaning, while Jewel collects the commission. That did not sit well with Ellen.

To make Ellen happy, Karen changed the rules. The new rules are posted. Elizabeth and Jewel have to accept them. Rules are as follows:

UPGRADE SHEET INFORMATION

To get 15% of any upgrade please do the following…

Write down the date, last name of guest, folio number (not confirmation number — the number of the in-house folio), room number, the rate total, pretax, and your initials.

The entire sheet MUST be filled before we "cash" it in,

So, upgrade, upgrade, upgrade…

** Upgrades are only applicable to Specialty Rooms or Suites sold at Rack Rate.

** Available only on any upgrade to a Specialty Room or Suite from a Standard village or Lake Room.

**Upgrade is not available if it creates any kind of in-house move.

**Not available with groups, packages, or any kind of discounted rates, (AARP or Military) and not available during Can/Am nor to CHE hockey groups)

Thank you and good luck!

Jewel's guest checked in for a two-night stay. The first night the guest stayed a night in a Standard Lakeside room.

The next day, the guest stops by Jewel's station.

"Good evening, Jewel. You checked me in last night and I'm enjoying my stay at this beautiful hotel."

"I'm very happy to hear that."

"I'm enjoying my stay so much I was wondering if I could upgrade to a Specialty suite?"

"Sure, let me check what's available."

Jewel checks Hotel Master. "Yes, we do have an upgrade for you with a fireplace and jetted tub."

"I'll take it!"

Jewel made the upgrade and switched him to the new room for one night. She posted her commission on the upgrade sheet.

The next day, Ellen finds out Jewel made commission on a one night move.

Ellen flipped out. She had to have the room cleaned and she's not making a commission. She marches into Karen's office crying. Hint, the reason for this new clause in the rules.

**Upgrades are not available if it creates any kind of in-*

house move.

Karen marches into the front desk clerk's back room and she scratches Jewel's upgrade off the Upgrade sheet. All to make Ellen happy. Not a word was spoken to Jewel about removing her commission. Jewel discovered that her commission was scratched off the sheet when she went into the back room and saw it. Everyone knows each upgrade made at the front desk makes Karen additional money.

Elizabeth and Jewel are fuming. Elizabeth thinks Karen plays favorites and she and Jewel are her least favorites. Even though Elizabeth and Jewel are making extra money for the hotel. Karen doesn't care. It's more important for Karen to keep Ellen happy.

Sports

Summertime is the busiest season of the year. The sunshine feels so comfortable on Jewel's skin as she walks down Main Street. The summer temperatures linger around 80 to 85 degrees without humidity. Main Street is bustling with large groups of entitled people coming through looking for a party.

The best part of the summer, of course, is Ironman. These people are serious athletes. They do not come for the parties. They cause no mayhem throughout the hotel. They wake up early, train, eat, rest, train, eat, repeat. These are extremely focused athletes.

This is the only time in the summer that the hotel is reasonably quiet. The clerks at the front desk get to meet lots of gentlemen, some of them are flirting.

Brenda and Jewel are working this evening. It's check in time. The hotel is completely booked up. This weekend is super busy with Ironman, the horse show, and a wedding.

"Good evening, may I help the next guest in line please?" Jewel asks.

"Yes, my name is Doug Anderson, I would like to check in. I am here for the triathlon."

"Yes, of course, Mr. Anderson. I'll retrieve your registration sheet."

Jewel returns with the sheet and does her usual check in spill.

"Are you participating in the triathlon, too?" Mr. Anderson asks.

"Oh no, I workout for myself so I can remain healthy and strong to live a longer life. I have no interest in competing."

"What are your sports of choice?"

"I'm a swimmer and a bike rider. I bike ride five times a week, six miles each time in the summer season and in the winter I swim at the local gym."

"Well, you do look healthy and strong. You're achieving your goals."

"Thank you, Mr. Anderson. Good luck this weekend! I'm sure I'll see you around before you leave."

"Yes, I'll be looking out for you. Enjoy your evening."

"Good night."

Mr. Anderson turns around and walks in the direction of his room.

The Ironman triathlon is 2.5 miles of swimming across

Mirror Lake, 112 miles of bike riding uphill in the Adirondack Mountains, and 26 miles of jogging all in a day. The Ironman may have to make a name change sooner than later. In 2022, American Sarah True along with Canadian Cody Beals were the winners. Women are winners, too. Ironwoman has a ring to it. Ironperson?

And then there is the Lake Avid Horse Show. Again, focused athletes. The one difference Jewel notices within these two groups is the horse show athletes are a little bit more entitled. They walk around with their noses up in the air. Ironman athletes are a little bit more down to earth. The horse show athletes wear Shad-bellies with a yellow vest, a traditional white stocked tie, and breeches. The sport of horse riding is high maintenance. It's an expensive sport. Ironman participants wear sneakers, bathing suits, shorts, and a tee-shirt. Only a bike is required. The athletes do purchase expensive bikes. Ironman athletes will pay thousands upon thousands of dollars for their bikes.

The Ironman event is a guaranteed booking for the hotel. Before the athletes check out of the hotel, they book their rooms for the upcoming year. Sometimes, the Ironman and Horse show events may overlap with wedding events. Leaving the Horse show participates with the leftover room; the Village side rooms.

Brenda and Jewel are working when a few horse riders come to check in during a super busy weekend.

It's 5:30 p.m.

"May I help the next person in line please?" Jewel asks.

A couple approaches her counter.

"Yes, I would like to check in."

"Yes, of course, may I have your name?"

"Larry Smith."

"One moment Mr. Smith, let me retrieve your registration sheet."

"Okay, thank you."

Jewel returns. She completes the check in and sends the couple along their way.

Five minutes later, Mr. Smith returns to Jewel's station.

"My wife is very unhappy with the room. Do you have anything on the Lakeside?"

"Mr. Smith, I'm pretty sure we are fully booked in the hotel, but let me double check for you."

"Thank you, please, anything you can do will be wonderful. My wife is very upset about the accommodation being on the Village side."

"I understand. Unfortunately, I do not see anything available for you, not even a Specialty suite. Let me go speak with the manager on duty, sometimes four eyes are better than two."

"Thank you, I greatly appreciate your help."

"You're welcome, one moment please."

Jewel turns to leave her work station, she opens the door to let herself out. She walks to Ginger's office. Ginger is sitting at her desk on her computer typing (tap, tap...) She's sucking on a lollipop, humming to herself.

"It smells like strawberries."

She looks up to see Jewel. She's in a good mood, Jewel notes.

Quickly, Ginger removes the lollipop out of her mouth.

"Oh, hi Jewel. Yeah, it's a strawberry lollipop. How are you? What's going on? How may I be of service to you?"

Ginger says jokily with a grin on her face. Jewel is thinking she must have gotten laid last night.

"Ginger, I have this couple who is participating in the horse show wanting to upgrade from the village side. I didn't see any place to move them. Please check for me."

"Well, isn't that bad luck for them."

Ginger begins typing (tap, tap, tap) in Hotel Master checking for availability.

"I see nothing. They'll have to stay where they are. I can offer them a full refund if they want to leave. Now let me get back to what I was doing."

"Thank you."

As Jewel turns around to leave Ginger's office, Ginger pops that lollipop back in her mouth and continues with her humming.

Jewel walks back to her station.

"Mr. Smith, I have spoken with my manager on duty and unfortunately there is just no place we can move you. She did offer to give you a full refund if you wish to leave."

Mr. Smith looks at Jewel with his puppy dog brown eyes and a frown on his face.

"I appreciate you trying."

"You're welcome, have a good evening."

Mr. Smith turns around slowly and walks away.

The lobby is quiet. Brenda and Jewel are speaking among themselves.

Minutes later, Mr. and Mrs. Smith are quickly approaching the front desk. Mrs. Smith is fuming, you can see the steam coming from her head. This time, they approach Brenda's station.

With a high pitched voice, Mrs. Smith asks Brenda, "May you please find me another room on the Lakeside?"

Mr. Smith walks away and heads to the bathroom.

Brenda starts laughing but at the same time she can see that this lady is pissed from the tone in her voice. Her laughter becomes soft.

"Yes, ma'am," says Brenda.

"Brenda, I spoke with Ginger." Jewel interjects herself into the conversation. "She checked. There aren't any rooms available on the Lakeside."

Mrs. Smith looks at Jewel with her hands on her hips. The tone in her voice became very degrading towards Jewel.

"I don't want your help! I'm not talking to you and I don't like your disposition! You have been nothing but a bitch since we arrived!"

Jewel grabs her chest and gasps for air, but says nothing. Obviously, the lady feels entitled.

Brenda intervenes to stop the escalation of the problem.

"Ma'am, I'll check for you!"

Brenda checks Hotel Master.

Jewel is called away. Minutes later, Jewel returns, walking slowly to her station from the South Direction. The Smiths' backs are turned to her. They can't see her coming.

Mrs. Smith is speaking to her husband in a high pitched

voice.

"I told that other Black woman off. I didn't like her disposition."

Mr. Smith says nothing. As Jewel approaches, Mrs. Smith shuts up.

Brenda is still standing there wasting time. Making believe a room is about to magically appear while nervously laughing. Jewel thinks, *"Is Brenda serious right now?"*

Brenda is twitching back and forth. Jewel is wondering if Brenda was about to "bust a move," but she speaks instead.

"Sorry, Mrs. Smith, there is no availability. I checked and I checked. I don't see anything."

They turn around and walk away with Mrs. Smith huffing and puffing and screaming at them. "I'm going to leave this hotel with the worst review. This is the worst customer service ever!"

Jewel felt like she was watching a bunch of two-year-olds. From the entitled Mrs. Smith throwing a temper tantrum in the lobby, to Brenda looking for a room that wasn't there.

As the season winds down, lacrosse is the last sporting event of the summer. The lacrosse athletes put Jewel in the mind of the hockey players. Young athletes with a great sportsmanship spirit causing havoc around the hotel. Young kids wandering around the hotel, not knowing where their parents are. The parents are at the Garden of Eden's bar, of course.

Jewel discovered that it's not illegal to leave your child home alone. She thought it was the law everywhere.

A family of four checks into the hotel. The first night of their stay, the parents go out for the evening and leave the two little children in the room. The siblings are as young as five and six years old. Well, one kid is in the room crying non stop for mommy. A complaint is made and the parents are called. The parents returned shortly afterwards. Everyone was talking about this incident at the front desk. Karen heard about it and that's how Jewel found out it was not against the law to leave the kids alone. Karen told them her parents left her and her siblings home alone all the time.

The Garden Tree Lakeside Resort offers several amenities. Included in the guest's stay: canoeing, water biking, kayaking, and Adam's wife performs a water show every Saturday evening. In the summertime, the beach is full of guests enjoying the amenities and the sun.

Another evening...

Brenda and Jewel are working. An elderly guest is staying in the hotel with her husband and a ten year old athletic grand boy. The grandmother approaches Brenda's station and starts whining to her.

"Ma'am, I'm here with my grandson for the lacrosse tournament and I'm relaxing on the beach while he has a quick swim before his game this evening. There's a lady on the beach with a bathing suit on that my grandson will not stop staring at. Can you please send someone to the beach and ask her to put on some clothes?"

Brenda laughs and looks at Jewel confused.

"Ma'am, the beach area is the place to wear a bathing suit. We cannot body shame anyone because your grandson is reaching puberty. I suggest you move to another side of the beach if you cannot control your grandson's glare."

The elderly guest is not pleased at Brenda's response. She replied, "Well, I have never been so insulted!"

She walks away and Brenda is still laughing.

Brenda looked at Jewel and said, "Can you believe that lady? Did she really just ask that I send someone outside and body shame one of the guests? Well, isn't she entitled! I wanted to call her "Karen" but my rent has to be paid this month."

Brenda and Jewel are both laughing now.

"Let's go look out the window and see if we can spot who she's talking about," says Jewel.

Brenda and Jewel walk to the window overlooking the beach, looking for this bombshell that had granny's panties in an uproar. They spot the bombshell. She had on a two piece red string bathing suit. Yes, she was showing a lot of ass. But again, America is a free country. Imagine all the women in the whole world looking the same. Everyone is a size four, all women are perfect. The world would be boring and people would find something else to complain about.

Weddings

Summertime is about the warm air and the sweet smell of love. And then come the weddings! The resort can have several weddings in a weekend. The wedding director is Jenny and her assistant is Amanda. They share an office within the hotel.

Elizabeth and Jewel are working. Weddings can be crazy! There's a wedding reception in the Tree House Ballroom this evening.

"Elizabeth, something strange is going on. Have you noticed people coming upstairs to use the restroom?"

"Yes, I have noticed."

There are six bathrooms closer to the Tree House Ballroom before coming up to the lobby. There should be no reason to come up the stairs to use the lobby's bathrooms.

"We should get to the bottom of this and figure out what's going on," Jewel says.

Elizabeth radioes Shawn, the houseman on duty.

"Shawn, please go see what's going on with the bathrooms near the Tree House. People have been coming up from the wedding party using the lobby's bathroom. Something must be wrong in the bathrooms near the Tree House

Ballroom."

"No problem. I'm on it."

Minutes later, Shawn radioes, "All the bathrooms have vomit in them."

Jewel picks the black radio up off the countertop. She presses on the side button and then she begins speaking.

"Ew, oh shit, there's no housekeeper on duty, Shawn."

"I'll take care of it, please make sure you log it in the shift report."

Jewel clicks on the radio button. "I'm typing it up right now. No worries."

It's not Shawn's job, but he cleaned all of those bathrooms. No one knew the reason for all the throwing up. It could have been bad food or a lot of guests drank too much.

This is a good reason handshakes should not be a thing. Now you have a bunch of drunk people going into the bathrooms, not washing their hands. We all know when men go into a bathroom to pee, some are handling their penis. Some don't wash their hands correctly, if at all. They walk out the bathroom and continue hugging and shaking people's hands. Just because you can't see the germs doesn't mean they're not on their hands. Some men enjoy rubbing their penis and then holding a beautiful woman. There are some creepy people in this world.

Another night…

Elizabeth and Jewel are working.

There must have been a full moon this evening.

Two different fights within the same night. Cops are called to the hotel each time.

A large, heavy weight, bodybuilder man, checked into the hotel. He had bulging muscles popping from his arms. He looks like a guy on steroids. He's huge! He has his bodybuilder girlfriend with him. They seem friendly enough at check in.

The phone rings, Elizabeth answers. "Hello, this is Elizabeth, how may I assist you?...Okay, okay, I'll be right there."

She hangs up the phone.

"I'll be right back, Jewel. I received a call about fighting on the second floor and a woman is screaming for help."

"Oh, boy here we go. Elizabeth, running to a fight is a bad idea," says Jewel. Every time Elizabeth receives a disturbance call, she runs to it. Jewel tells her it's dangerous but Elizabeth never listens. Off she goes.

Elizabeth returns quickly and dials 911.

"Please send someone quickly to the Garden Tree Lakeside Resort on Main Street. There's a man in the hotel arguing with this woman. It's very loud and she's screaming for help. I'm afraid he may hurt her."

Elizabeth pauses and is listening.

"He's a White male, bodybuilder looking guy with huge muscles. Around 30-ish years old, staying in room 224 on the second floor."

Jewel is listening to Elizabeth. Elizabeth paused to listen to the operator.

"Thank you. I hear them coming now. Good night."

Elizabeth hangs up.

The cops enter into the building and Elizabeth quickly escorts them to room 224. Upon arrival at the room's door the police bang and bang on the door.

"It's the police, open the door! Open the door now!"

The big muscled man opens the door. The police enter the room. "What's going on?" The lady is sitting on the floor, crying uncontrollably.

The muscle man explains, "It was just an argument. I didn't do anything."

The police handcuff the man and they exit the room.

Elizabeth reports back to Jewel. When she entered the room behind the officers, she noticed that the toilet was detached from the floor and in pieces. The lady was crying and screaming that the man had done it. Elizabeth couldn't believe it.

The next day...

Karen charged the guest accordingly for the damage. In the past, guests have ripped the wall-mounted television off and smashed it on the floor. Beds have been flipped over and left outside on the patio. People will trash a hotel. The costs are billed to the guest. Karen is paid. Guests would get hit with an extra $1,000.00 added to their room's bill. She would kick them out of the hotel for the damages and then she'd blacklist them on their profile in Hotel Master.

On that same night, there was another disturbance call. A different couple that got married in the hotel over the weekend. Jewel answered the phone this time. The lady from room 105 is calling. Her husband hit her. He had been drinking and they got into an argument.

She asked, "Can someone please call the police?"

Jewel makes the call to 911.

A few minutes later, her husband's in the lobby, obviously drunk, yelling at a man. A physical fight breaks out. The cops have arrived. The fight is broken up. The men are handcuffed and thrown in the patrol cars.

Guests never call the police themselves. They call the front desk first and ask them to call the police. Even in a life or death situation.

This evening, Brenda and Jewel are working together.

Jewel sees an overweight lady running towards her. Jewel can hear how heavy she is breathing from the little bit of exercise she just experienced.

Heavily breathing, she is screaming out at Jewel.

"Please help me! Call 911!"

Jewel calmly replies, "Okay ma'am, what's wrong?"

She's now standing in front of Jewel at her station trying to catch her breath.

Jewel is holding the phone in her right hand and using her left pointer finger to dial 911 as the lady is catching her breath.

While she is huffing and puffing. "My daughter is having an allergic reaction to something. Her body has bumps all over it and her lips are swollen."

"911 operator, what's your emergency?"

"Hi, can you please send an ambulance to the Garden Tree Lakeside Resort on Main Street? A minor guest is having an allergic reaction to something."

"I have dispatched the ambulance and they're en route to your location. What's the child's name and age?"

The mother has calmed down, so Jewel attempts to hand

her the phone. The cord is too short to reach over the counter. Jewel is thankful, she didn't want to deal with the transfer of germs to her phone.

"Ma'am, the operator would like to know your daughter's name and age?"

"Emily is 16. Are they on their way? How long will it be before they get here?" The mother replies frantically.

"Emily is 16 years old." Jewel lets the operator know.

The sound of a siren is closing in from a distance.

"I hear them coming now."

"Ma'am, please remain on the line with me until they have arrived."

"Yes, of course. They're pulling in the parking lot now. The mother has run outside to greet them."

"Okay then you have a good evening."

"Thank you. You too."

The line is disconnected. The paramedics are following the mother towards her room.

Five minutes later, the young Emily, and her mother, along with the paramedics get in the ambulance and they drive away.

Elizabeth, Brenda and Jewel are very social. To work with the public everyday, you should like people. They speak to everyone. Brenda and Jewel are working. An elderly lady in her 60's stops at the front desk everyday to speak. A beautiful olive skin toned woman with thick, dark brown, wavy hair. She's a Jewish mother from Long Island. She's staying in the hotel for her child's wedding.

Most evenings of her five night stay, she spent time talking with the front desk staff. She's lonely. She's divorced. She talks and talks. She's been excited about her gift of Maison Marcel Rose, a limited edition wine. A gift she will give the couple.

During the week, the staff meets her children and the in-laws. Brenda is even hired to babysit the lady's grand baby at the wedding. Brenda is excited; they offered her $250.00 for several hours. Brenda and Jewel have several laughs with the lady while getting to know her.

One evening, the Jewish mother is standing stationed next to Jewel talking about her ex.

"You know we were married for 35 years and have five children. He came home one day and told me he wanted a divorce. I took him to the cleaners. He'll be here tomorrow with his younger girlfriend. She's from Venezuela. My family and I call her, "Toast."

Jewel looks surprised as she turns and looks at Brenda who is also confused.

"Toast?" Jewel asks the older woman. "What do you

mean?"

Looking Jewel in the eye, she says, "She's your complexion."

Pure racism! People are so comfortable thinking about discrimination in their own heads, when it came out of her mouth it was natural to her. She was as comfortable as one can be with themselves. It was like she just took a good ass shit. No, no, it was like she didn't see that Brenda and Jewel are Black. She didn't see anything wrong with calling them, "Toast."

Jewel looks at Brenda again. She then looks at the lady in disbelief.

The lady continued, "No one in the family likes her."

This lady is obviously jealous of her ex-husband's new girlfriend. To give herself some power, she belittles the new girlfriend. The thing that's a pickle; the lady has an olive tone complexion herself. She is a woman of color. She failed to realize her ex-husband probably knows she a racist. She has no soul. She came to the lobby every evening, laughing and joking with Brenda and Jewel but she was only doing it to fill her void of loneliness. She is a lady who's a black sheep walking around in women's clothes. He went looking for a woman with a soul. That is why he chose an ethnic woman.

The next day, her family keeps staring at Jewel and Brenda. They're just looking and looking.

"Brenda, do you see this family keeps staring at us?"

"Yes, I noticed. She must have told them she mistakenly called the two Black ladies at the front desk "toast.""

"I'm going to have to agree with you, Brenda."

Its check in time: 4:00 p.m.

"May I help the next guest in line, please?" Brenda asks while laughing.

"Yes, my name is Elijah Abrams. I'm here with my girlfriend for the wedding this weekend."

Brenda laughs and says, "Welcome! It's nice to have both of you here staying with us."

Jewel takes note that Brenda has an attractive older gentleman, who appears to be in his late 60's at her station. His girlfriend is stunning, she looks like she's in her late 40s, maybe early 50s. She has long dark, natural flowing curls, with beautiful soft olive skin. She is well put together with make up on her face and heels on her feet.

"Thank you," the girlfriend says with an accent.

Mr. Abrams is finishing up the registration sheet.

"I noticed you have an accent. Where are you from?" Brenda asks.

"I'm from Venezuela."

Brenda turns and looks at Jewel. She hopes Jewel was listening because this is the ex-husband and girlfriend of the lady who called them "toast."

Mr. Abrams looks up at Brenda as he lays the pen down on the countertop and hands her the registration sheets.

"I have a question. I need help with something."

With a big grin on her face. "Yes, of course Mr. Abrams, how may I assist you?"

"I have rented a car for the weekend but will be flying out of the area on Sunday. I'm willing to pay a couple of hundred dollars for anyone who's willing to return the car for me to Hertz in Plattsburgh. Do you know of anyone?"

"I'll be happy to do that for you Mr. Abrams. I'm off on Sunday," Brenda says, still amused by the situation.

"Thank you. Please meet me here at 11:00 a.m. Will that be okay?"

Laughing, laughing, laughing...

"No problem."

"Thank you so much. You're a lifesaver!"

Laughing, laughing, laughing...

"It was nice meeting you guys. Please press 0 from your room phone if you need any assistance. Jewel and I will be here working for the evening."

"Good evening."

The couple leaves Brenda's station and walks in the direction of their room.

Brenda turns to Jewel. "Jewel, that was the ex-husband and his girlfriend from Venezuela."

"Yes, I heard the conversation. She is a beautiful young lady. It's obvious why the ex-wife is jealous."

Brenda has a big smile on her face.

"They are really nice people. This weekend between babysitting and now returning the car, I'm going to be making some good money."

Brenda's laughing and laughing.

"That is so cool. Congratulations, get that money, lady," Jewel says with a big smile on her face.

An hour or so later, the ex-wife shows up to the front desk. She came bearing gifts in her hand. She has two bottles of Maison Marcel Rose. One bottle in each hand. A bottle for Brenda and one for Jewel. They accept. Jewel never turns down a free bottle of anything that has some alcohol in it. But the reality of the situation is that there is now a confirmed group of racist people staying in the hotel.

Jewish women can be so extra with their entitlement.

Some walk around as if they're superior. The biggest haters in the world are "Karens." Another race of women couldn't be doing better in life than a Jewish woman without her feeling jealous. No congratulations from a jealous woman, just pure hate.

Their envy can run so deep into jealousy and that jealousy can become hate. Reason for the term HATERS! Haters are weak insecure people who don't know who they are or what they want, so they want everything someone else has. It's sad, but that's what this lady was dealing with, hating on her ex-husband's girlfriend. These are dangerous types of people. As soon as Jewel realizes she's in the presence of one of these evil people she stays far away from them.

Jewel has run into a few racist people in the community. Especially when she operated her health food store. The Garden Tree felt like a safe place from a lot of that. Karen didn't give off much of a racist vibe. Well, sometimes Jewel was gullible. Jena from the NYC gym was an example of that.

One day, Jewel's working a double starting with the morning shift at 7:00 a.m. She was filling in for Stella. Stella is out sick, again. Mary and Jewel are working together. A gay, black, tall, slim, male houseman named Joe got into an altercation. He was assisting a guest with his luggage. The guest was a White, middle aged man. Jewel recognized him from his stay. During his stay he'd come to Jewel's station for small talk. He seemed nice enough.

Joe comes to the front desk crying, "Mary, may I speak

with you in the back room please?"

"Yes, of course, Joe."

At this point, Mary is six months pregnant. She plops out of the chair. The pregnancy wobble is present in her steps as she strolls to the back room.

She returns and says, "Jewel, I'll be back." She exits the front desk station and heads towards Karen's office. Joe goes back to work. Karen comes out of her office with Mary. They walked to the window overlooking the parking lot. Jewel can't hear their conversation. Mary is pointing her finger at a car. Mary returns to her station. Karen continues to stand at the window as if she was waiting for someone. Jewel is curious.

"Mary, what's going on?"

Mary lifts her left pointer finger and puts it on her lips.

"Shh!" Mary whispers. "That guest that just checked out called Joe the "N" word."

"Oh," Jewel replies.

Mary continues, "Karen is waiting for him to return to his car."

And she waited and she waited for about 15 minutes before he returned. Karen goes outside and they have words in the parking lot. Mary and Jewel don't know what is said but the conversation went on for about 10 minutes. Karen comes back into the hotel and returns to her office. She doesn't ask to speak with Joe and she doesn't blacklist the guest from returning to the hotel.

A German family had a wedding at the hotel. The German pianist invited to the wedding would hang out at the front desk with Brenda and Jewel. A talented, middle aged, White man. He told them stories about Germany. He didn't get to see many Black people where he was from.

He explained, "When a Black person would be seen riding a bike down the street. There was always interest in the air about the person. The people became very curious about who was riding the bike and where did he/she come from."

He also told them it's against the law to say the "N" word in Germany. He said if a German person was caught saying the word "Nigger" they could be arrested.

Brenda and Jewel are very surprised by this information. They turn to one another, look each other in the eyes and then turn back to continue looking at him.

His stories remind Jewel of Karen speaking to one of the guest about calling Joe the houseman a nigger.

This German pianist left a review for Brenda and Jewel. It reads as follows:

The front desk staff were rude and not so friendly for the exception of the African American ladies. Those two ladies were super friendly and helpful. They made us feel welcomed and at home.

The Marketing Manager, Judy, replies. *Sorry, you didn't have a good experience with the front desk.*

Nothing positive was said from Judy about Brenda and Jewel. She failed to comment about the positive experience the guest had at the front desk with them. Judy only focused on the negative comments.

Things People Say That Make You Go Hmmm

1. Does the elevator go up?
2. "Pounding the pints," a hockey kid said to his dad.
3. Do not make the fart bigger than the ass.
4. It's July. The question, "Can we ice skate outdoors?"
5. You have a young person's face, with an old lady's hair style.
6. I'll see you around, like a donut.
7. We all have to be a wheel and move forward.
8. The crack of my ass is itching.
9. Let me zip your fly.
10. May I touch your hair?
11. "Fuck off!" a hockey kid said to his mom.
12. "My mother told me I don't have to answer to the help." a hockey kid said to the staff.

AUTUMN

Autumn and the Leaf Peepers

J ewel's favorite season of the year is autumn. The vibrant colors of red, orange and yellow leaves bring cheers throughout the community. Jewel noticed smiles on faces as she walks down Main Street. The Adirondacks offer fresh, crisp mountain air for breathing. It's time to pull the jackets and sweaters out of the closet. Halloween, Thanksgiving and apple cider are coming. Jewel has excitement building up from the change of the season.

The J1's have left for the summer season. Karen sent out her usual email asking for additional help in the laundry and/or housekeeping department. In addition to the help needed in those two departments, the Leaf Peepers are coming.

The Leaf Peepers are elderly, retired, white Americans traveling via a chartered bus. They travel throughout the North Country's picturesque communities like Lake Avid in search of the autumn foliage. The tour includes a bus driver, a tour guide, and accommodation for a seven-night stay. Food not included.

A sheet is posted behind the front desk clerks' back room. The sheet includes the date and time of the arrival and departure of the Leaf Peepers. This is Jewel's first year at the hotel, so when she sees the sheet she is confused. The sheet reads as follow:

LUGGAGE RULES
PLEASE READ BEFORE SIGNING UP

- You must punch in and out while doing luggage.
- You must not be scheduled to work for the same shift you are doing luggage for.
- Bags in will require 2 people (For better customer service).
- Bags out should require only one.
- If you haven't done luggage before, please see Ginger before your first bus.
- All payouts will be done after the departure of the last bus of the season.

The payout is $6.00 ($3.00 per person per bag)

$3.00 per bag out

$3.00 goes to HSPK

$9.00 total.

Attached to the rules is the "Bus Baggage Sign Up Sheet,"
ten buses in and ten buses out. Out of the twenty spots,
Jewel signs up for fourteen of them. She is scheduled to
work during the other six spots.

Jewel spoke with Ginger. Ginger explained to Jewel the
details of the job. She tells her some of the luggage is very
heavy and large. Jewel is up for a challenge. She's getting
paid to workout, that's a win win for Jewel.

Ginger continued to explain.

"You have to use the hotel bell cart to deliver each person's
luggage to their room. You'll be provided a list of the
guests' names with their room number. Whoever is
working the front desk at the time of the bus' arrival will
provide the room keys. They are programmed and inserted
into the key packet before they enter the lobby."

The first bus arrives. Jewel walks outside to retrieve a hotel
bell cart and approaches the bus. The driver unloads the
luggage onto the pavement. She checks the luggage tags
for the name. She writes the room number on each tag.
She puts the luggage heading to the same floor on a cart
together. She fills each cart up and pushes one by one. She
drops the luggage off in front of each guest's room.

It can take up to an hour for a small group and two hours
for a bigger group. It's a lot of work. There would be days
Jewel would have to be at the hotel at 6:00 a.m. A bus had
to be loaded and ready to go at 7:00 a.m. The Leaf Peepers
sit their luggage outside their room's door. Jewel grabs
them and throws the luggage onto the cart. Collecting the

luggage is an easier job to do than delivering to their rooms.

Jewel is the only person in the hotel who is interested in doing the job. Brenda signed up for a couple of buses. Ginger and Stella worked together on one bus. Amanda from the wedding department took a bus. People looked down on the job. Jewel on the other hand, she took pride. She was becoming physically stronger from the hard work. Jewel would see Karen giving her the side eye while she pushed a cart full of luggage.

"Karen thinks she's too good to do the luggage," Jewel thought.

Jewel believes in real hard work for an honest day's pay. Employees will waste time playing around and not doing their jobs. Jewel watches employees work for only an hour before taking their lunch breaks. It's sad but very common in the workplace. It's called stealing time from the business. Jewel never steals time. When she is on the clock she works for her money.

Upon completion of the Leaf Peeper's bus project; Jewel banked an extra $1,300.00 in tips. In the same week's pay, her upgrade check posted an extra $800.00. Jewel's check was $3,000.00 for the week. In addition to her regular pay she had overtime in laundry which totaled up to a 60 hours work week. The IRS took 35 percent out of her check. She felt like a slave, working for free.

The following week, Karen spent time helping Jewel in laundry, it was a first. She was folding towels and helping

Chandler with the sheets. She asked Jewel questions about the correct way to fold the towels. Jewel explained everything that she does while working in the laundry department. For example, Jewel didn't know how to fold the sheets correctly, so when she finished with all the towels, she would then fold pillowcases. This let Karen know time isn't wasted while Jewel waits for the towels to finish drying. She knew how to use the washer and dryers, too. While Chandler and Jack are working she would load up the washing machine and dryers to help move things along quickly. Gloves are worn while loading up the washing machines and hands washed when finished.

Even Chandler is surprised Karen is helping in laundry. He said it was a first in his twenty-eight years of working with the family. Jewel is not sure if she's being watched. Jewel earned lots of money while the J1's were away. Becky started helping out in the housekeeping department, too. Jewel hopes they are not spying on her. All the staff knows Jewel is a very hard working person and earns all of her money.

At the end of the day when Karen was ready to head home, Jewel thanked her for the help. The laundry department is always backed up and Jewel worked long hours trying to help them get ahead. It's very helpful to have extra hands in the laundry department during staff shortage. Chandler let her know he was thankful, too.

When the J1's are away, she'd work 60-hour weeks non stop. However, between the Leaf Peeper's luggage and overtime, Jewel is becoming super tired. She is busy all the time. She doesn't have time for fun or any social entertainment. She did enjoy working. Jewel is happy staying busy. She has no man and she lives alone.

It's a cold, autumn evening with temperatures in the 20's. Brenda and Jewel are working this evening. It's 10:30 p.m. and a man rushes into the lobby. He tells Brenda and Jewel that his car has broken down in the hotel parking lot. He needs a jump. The problem is there's a car in the parking lot in his way. The car parked in his way belongs to a guest in the hotel.

"Can you please call the guest's room and ask them to move their car?" He asks.

"Sorry Sir," Brenda says, laughing. "I'm not calling the guest due to the late hour."

Brenda radioes Shawn to come help. For emergency purposes, Karen keeps a portable car jumper starter in her office. Shawn goes into Karen's office to retrieve the machine. He takes it outside and instructs the man after he is finished to please return it to the front desk. While all this is going on, Ronnie arrives for his shift. Shawn returns to the lobby and approaches the front desk and tells them everything that is going on.

"You have to stay outside with the man," Ronnie says. "You have to make sure the man doesn't leave with the machine."

"It's too cold outside," Shawn refuses. "I'm not doing that."

They continue the argument back and forth. Shawn finally walks away.

That was just the beginning…

The next evening…

Elizabeth and Jewel are working this time. The shift is wrapping up and Ronnie walks into the lobby fuming. Ronnie walking into the front door lobby is rare. It has never happened before. Ronnie always enters the hotel from the Devine Mall entrance. The Devine Mall entrance is two doors down from his apartment.

When Ronnie enters through the Devine Mall, he locks the mall's double doors behind him. That's usually around 11:00 p.m. The Devine Mall doors are supposed to be locked every night at 10:00 p.m. by the houseman that is on shift. Tonight, Shawn is on duty. He takes it upon himself to lock up the Devine Mall's doors before Ronnie's arrival.

"Who locked the mall doors?" Ronnie screams as he comes through the front doors. Brenda and Jewel look at each other in confusion.

Assuming it was Shawn, Brenda radioes him.

Shawn explains. "When I was hired, I was told to lock up the Devine mall at 10:00 p.m. The same time I lock up the pool and gym."

Well, this is a first, he hasn't locked the door before tonight.

Shawn reaches the front desk. Shawn and Ronnie go at it and a big argument explodes in the lobby. The issue reaches management and Ronnie is forced to apologize to Shawn. Shawn is told to continue locking the door at 10:00 p.m.

Ronnie shift report read:

- *Havoc before the holidays!*
- *Have a splendid day, and stay safe!*

A month goes by and autumn turns into winter. Ronnie is still entering the hotel through the front door after several years of working at the resort.

Another day…

Ginger is spending time with the married Electrum man. Something is going on with the phones, televisions, and Wi-Fi in the hotel and the technician is here to fix it. Karen finally addresses the issue with the front desk.

Email received from Karen:

Hi FD Team,

Well, if it's not one thing it is another. Phones are basically fixed (85% percent anyway) and now the TVs are freaking out. Many of the TVs in the South wing are not working. They say no signal. We have tried everything and Adam or Chad has changed everything so they think an AMP may be dead.

Rumor is the Amp will be delivered by Monifi (cable company) on Monday - WHEN IT ARRIVES PLEASE PUT IT IN MY OFFICE SO IT'S EASY TO FIND.

On Wednesday, both Electrum and Monifi will be coming here. Please call Chad when they arrive at 518-555-****, so he can show them whatever they need to see.

There is a guy coming this afternoon (Saturday) to meet with Adam, but without Amps it is not likely there is anything he can do. We will see.

In the meantime, if people freak out about no TVs, please explain we have been working on it for two days but we're at the mercy of the TV companies. I have told Can/Am that we may be offering people a 10% discount off the room rate if they really can't handle watching shows on their iPads. So, if a guest is losing their mind — you can offer them 10% off the room rate but explain to them the refund will come from Can/Am sometime next week. AND THEN YOU MUST LEAVE GINGER A SHIFT NOTE EXPLAINING SO SHE CAN ADJUST THE BILL.

If someone is really freaking out — they can move to room 127. I just checked and the TV in there works.

The TV in 346 does not work.

Sorry about this guys. We are doing our best to fix it as quickly as possible.

Karen.

It's Ronnie's night off. Ava (who covers Ronnie's shift the two nights a week he has off) is releasing Elizabeth and Jewel from their shift. This turns out to be a bad night for Ava. Ava has anxiety to the point it affects her breathing. In the past, she has called Ginger in the middle of the night to come release her because of her anxiety.

The next night, Jewel and the ladies found out the police called the front desk. They were looking for a dog friendly hotel. The hotel is dog friendly, so Ava let the officer know.

Ten minutes later...

The police officer arrived with a drunk, white American male and his dog. Ava does her standard check in spill and the process goes well. The drunk man heads in the North direction to his room.

An hour later...

A little after midnight, a guest approaches Ava station to tell her there's a man masturbating in his room with the door open. Ava didn't know what to do, so she called Ronnie and asked him for help.

Ronnie arrives at the hotel and kicked the man out of the building. He, himself, witnessed the man masturbating with the door open. That guest and his dog were never seen again.

Ronnie's shift report:

- *Maybe someone should inform the police that we are a*

LAKESIDE RESORT. The police should be taking the homeless to the Motel Inn.

- *Management: block the man that was in room 305 in Hotel Master.*

- *Thank God no children were around while this creep was in the hotel causing havoc.*

Hotel versus Airbnb

J ewel is at home dancing and singing around her apartment. She's in a great mood. She pulled her clothes out of her drawer and closet. Singing loudly Beyonce's "America has a problem," while folding her clothes into tiny pieces. She packs a lite bag. A few bathsuits, a wetsuit, some shorts, panties, a dress and flip flop. She keeps her bag lite enough to store under the plane seat. Jewel doesn't want to pay the baggage fees the airline charges. She doesn't like checking in her luggage due to the airline losing her luggage in the past.

Jewel's vacation to Belize is coming up quickly. In anticipation of her upcoming trip she has to decide if she'll be staying in a hotel or an Airbnb. Certain factors come into play when Jewel decides if she'll stay in a hotel or an Airbnb when traveling. Jewel makes her decision based on the number of nights of her stay, the number of people traveling with her, and her destination.

If Jewel is going on a short trip; for example, a two-night stay- she'll stay in a hotel. If it's more than a two-night stay she'll stay in an Airbnb. Safety also plays an important part in her decision on where to stay, especially when traveling internationally. Some countries are not recommended for travel. There are certain countries Jewel will not go to for example, Russia and Haiti. Jewel tries to stay out of countries that are known for kidnapping Americans and war.

When traveling for long stays in another country, people usually stay more than two nights. Jewel stays in an Airbnb so she can cook her own meals. If you decide to stay in an Airbnb, make sure it's a condo and not a free standing house. Condos usually offer security. Most condos are gated with a security guard present. Culture is very important when it comes to security. If you're traveling to Puerto Rico and your security guard is Russian and not Puerto Rican you should ask someone about that.

Jewel always checks the reviews before booking her stay at a new place. Airbnb has a super host program which makes it easy to narrow down the best accommodations for the vacation area.

Hotels have all kinds of amenities, and if you don't see something you want, ask for it. Guests are really not entitled to much more than what the hotel offers. In reality, each guest is entitled to basic accommodations, for example running hot and cold water, towels, and a bed. Of course each guest wants to arrive at a hotel and all their desires are met. For example, when a guest approaches the front desk, you would hope the clerk will greet all guests with a warm smile. However, the front desk is not entitled to put on a smile for each guest. The front desk clerk's job is to check you in, tell you how to navigate your way around the hotel, and not to be rude.

Some people travel a very long distance to get to their vacation destination and upon arrival, their attitude may suck. The sucky attitude usually comes from them being tired and hungry. There are also the people that arrive who are super excited to get their vacation started. When Jewel travels she enjoys the culture of the people within the country she's in. Hotels are full of tourists, usually American. Jewel thinks she could have stayed at home in America if her accommodations were to be around a bunch of Americans.

Jewel has experience running her own Airbnb in her apartment in NYC. The laws have changed from time to time in NYC for Airbnbs. When people started running Airbnbs, you could have guests stay daily or weekly. Now the law has changed to monthly. Airbnbs are also frowned upon due to long term tenants complaining of things like noise. So, Jewel was running an illegal Airbnb in her apartment.

She would charge up to $200.00 a night for guests to stay in her apartment. Finally, when the landlord got wind of Jewel making cash from the apartment, a deal was put into place to get her out. Jewel received enough money to afford a place in Lake Avid. At this point Jewel had enough money saved to pay a year's rent in advance and put money on a downpayment for the health food store.

Hotels, Airbnb, real estate, anything that has to do with property value from Jewel's experience is the most profitable field of business there is. Money, money, money will always be made in most real estate dealings.

Jewel Vacations Alone

Jewel has landed in Belize City, Central America, filled with excitement to the point of tears. Her plan for this trip is pure relaxation. She wants to hang out with the locals and stay as far away from Americans as she can. Jewel is traveling alone to Placencia, Belize. Placencia is a sixteen mile peninsula south of Belize City. Jewel must state the obvious; it's so hot she feels like she's close to the devil.

Upon Jewel's arrival to Belize City, she catches a twenty-five minute flight to Placencia. Upon arrival at Placencia Airport, Jewel goes outside to grab a taxi. There is one taxi outside, but he already has a pre-arranged passenger to pick up. He asks Jewel to wait fifteen minutes for his return. While Jewel is waiting, another taxi arrives but she turns him down. The fifteen minutes goes by and then twenty minutes goes by and the taxi hasn't returned yet.

Jewel goes back to the man standing around looking for passengers.

"Sir if you don't mind, may I get that ride?"

He is using his right pointer finger pointing at himself to confirm Jewel is speaking to him.

"Me?" The driver asks.

"Yes, you Sir."

The driver walks off to get his taxi and he asks Jewel to wait for him. Moments later, when he returns, he's driving a broken down green Dodge caravan. Jewel noted how bad this taxi looked. The rust has eaten parts of the green away from the caravan. The rust had caused holes throughout and around the van.

The remaining passengers standing around waiting for their rides are looking in horror for Jewel.

The driver gets out of the van and walks over to the other side to open the sliding door for Jewel to enter. She climbs in the taxi with her baggage which she throws on the empty seat next to herself.

"Ma'am, keep the door open so you can get a breeze."

"Okay."

As the taxi is traveling along the two-mile ride to her Airbnb it breaks down.

"Oh shoot," the driver says. "I'll have it fixed quickly. We will be moving along in a moment."

Jewel is nervous because of recent reports of Americans being kidnapped in the Caribbean. She can also hear her friend, the coach, telling her to be careful traveling to the Caribbean alone.

"Okay, Sir."

The driver gets out of the caravan and goes to fix the problem. He lifts the hood and pulls something out of the engine that looks like a black box and throws it in the back of the van.

"I'll put it back together later," the driver conveys to Jewel.

He gets back in the caravan, turns the ignition on, and continues along the route for about a half of a mile or so. That is until a speed bump comes upon them and then the caravan stalls again. This time it stalls in a wooded area. All kinds of things are running through Jewel's mind.

"Oh boy, is this where they're going to kidnap me?" Jewel asks herself.

"No worries, ma'am." He jumps out and walks in front of the caravan and lifts the hood.

"Sir, how much further do we have to go? Can I walk?"

"No, we still have a mile to go." He turns, pointing his right pointer finger away from Jewel, showing her the direction they will be continuing this ride.

"Sir, you shouldn't pick passengers up if you don't have a working vehicle," Jewel remarks to the driver annoyingly.

"I apologize. We will be out of here shortly."

Finally, another taxi stops and offers to help. Jewel jumps out of the taxi quickly and heads to the other taxi.

"Hey, hey wait, you have to pay me!"

"What? You didn't take me to my destination."

Both the men start speaking in Spanish to each other.

"Okay, I paid him, so you pay me."

"No, problem."

Jewel hands over the money and jumps into the modern day silver Dodge caravan.

The driver gets in the caravan, too and then he pulls off onto the road. As they're driving along the route, Jewel shares her frustration with the driver. "I have no idea why that guy would pick up passengers in a vehicle that keeps breaking down."

"Well, he's trying to feed his family like the rest of us." For the next two minutes there's silence in the vehicle. "We're here. Enjoy your stay in Belize."

"Thank you, Sir."

Jewel grabs her belongings, gives him a tip, and exits the caravan.

Upon arrival at the Airbnb, Jewel's host is standing outside waiting. She gives Jewel the quick lay of the land. Jewel is very hungry so she quickly gets herself settled in and heads out in search of food, beer, and the beach. She runs upon Mexican Belizean food, it looks interesting. She orders three chicken Pilsen which came to $4.50 BLZ which is double American currency. Jewel is shocked. In America you cannot get lunch for $2.50. Jewel is in such disbelief of the prices that she hasn't moved to actually pay. Getting annoyed, the clerk keeps confirming the price.

"Yes, like it says on the board."

Jewel replies, "Okay, I'll leave you alone."

That interaction reminded Jewel of when working at the hotel during wedding season. The wedding department always posts a sign in front of the entrance directing the wedding guests where to go. The majority of the guests walk right by the sign, approach the front desk, and ask for directions. The front desk staff find this to be very annoying. No matter where they put the sign, the guests refuse to stop and read. This is how Jewel discovered that the majority of people in the world do not like to read. She was able to relate to the Belizean young man being a little annoyed. But in her defense, she is in another country.

Belize is a melting pot of people from all over the world. It reminds Jewel of where she was born; Queens. There are several different languages spoken here as well, the language that she hears the most besides English is Creole. The way the locals explained it to Jewel is that Creole was the language of the slaves. It's the English language, but spoken in a way the slave masters couldn't understand. Jewel found this to be so interesting because she's hanging out with about six local black guys and she's the only person who doesn't understand Creole. She didn't want to be compared to a slave master, so she tried to catch on as quickly as she could.

As the men are talking, Jewel is listening intensely.

"You can understand the words he is saying," one guy says. "Break it down slowly, for you to understand. We are speaking fast, making it difficult for the 'masters' to understand."

"Okay, I'm slowly getting it," Jewel says. "I'll have to come back with my daughter and spend more time with you guys."

"Oh yes, bring your beautiful daughter here. I want to marry her."

Jewel burst out laughing. "You don't even know my daughter. "

"That's okay, we can get to know each other."

"I'll have to let her know a stranger wants to propose to her. I'll see you guys tomorrow. I'm going to get my dinner now."

Jewel gets up to leave.

"Bye, see you later."

Jewel waves bye.

When Jewel travels to these unique areas of the world it's because of the culture and the food. This is how Jewel learns more and more about herself. Jewel takes great pride in being a black American woman. However, when she travels to such countries as Belize, she is easily reminded that her culture is the culture of America, White America.

On the second day of Jewel's twelve-night stay, she has goals. She wants to hook up with the weed guys and stay on the beach and of course, eat. She gets all goals accomplished and then dinner time comes. Jewel does get the whole relaxed vibe but this was on a whole other level. She goes to a restaurant located on the beach. She seats herself, but it's not the best beach view. But...the waiter takes Jewel's order. She ordered a Red Stripe beer, water, and buttered garlic shrimp with mash potatoes and veggies. The waiter is not doing his job. He's hanging out at the bar with a woman. You know the rest of the world thinks Americans do not have much patience?

The restaurant has very few guests. Jewel is the fourth occupied table. The two tables closest to the beach are occupied and a very large family has the center of the floor with several tables pulled together to accommodate their size. Jewel is seated in a booth between each group. The table closest to Jewel gets up and heads to the bar. She gets tired of waiting, because there is only one waiter and he is spending his shift flirting with a lady at the bar. The lady who got up to head to the bar ordered drinks for her table. Jewel already watched her table place their order with the waiter. The waiter had not put in any orders for drinks. Jewel is watching him flirt, contemplating if she too should get up and go order her drink as well. Jewel is not used to this "no service" at a sit down restaurant. She is slightly confused.

While all this is going on, the large family leaves and shortly afterward one of the tables closest to the beach becomes available. Now there are a few dirty tables and Jewel has her eye set on the table closest to the beach. When Jewel finally gets the waiter's attention, she asks to switch tables so she may be closer to the beach. The waiter replies, "Primo," and he walks away.

Jewel sits and drinks her Red Stripe beer which she finally decided to retrieve for herself. The waiter decides to clean the largest group tables before cleaning the table that Jewel requested. After he cleans all those tables he brings Jewel her food. The waiter is now back with the girl at the bar, not thinking about cleaning the table that she requested. He finally slowly gets to cleaning the requested table, but she is enjoying her food at the moment and by the time the table is completely clean Jewel has finished eating.

He approaches Jewel and asks if everything is okay. She looks at him as if he is crazy. She's thinking, "*This really doesn't matter. I'll show my love and appreciation in his tip.*"

"Primo, may I have the check?" Jewel asks.

"Yes, one moment, ma'am."

"*I hope it doesn't take as long to get this check as it did to get my beer, which I got for myself,*" Jewel is thinking.

Jewel has her eyes on the waiter because she didn't plan to spend the night at this restaurant. He's walking over to her.

"Here is your check. Thank you for dining with us this evening."

"You're welcome," Jewel says as she grabs a hold of the check.

Jewel is scanning the check with her eyes. *"Is this real?"*

In addition to his horrible customer service he doesn't know how to add. It was $24.00BZL for the garlic shrimp and $7.50BZL for the Red Stripe beer. She didn't receive the water ordered. Jewel's bill total came to $24.75BZL. Jewel is going through it, the shock of it all.

"How can he have this job and he can't do simple math?"

Unlike with the conversation she had with the Mexican Belizean, Jewel keeps her mouth closed. The waiter's customer service was so poor Jewel thought he was giving away free beer. After the bill was settled, she left the waiter a $2.00 tip. Worst customer service ever, but the food was so so good.

When a person goes to a restaurant, they expect basic service. For example, having their drinks brought to their table. That's the part of the customer service that should be a given when sitting at a table for dinner at a restaurant. This reminds Jewel of her visit to the Garden of Flower when Shannon didn't want to blow dry Black women's hair.

Speaking of Shannon, Jewel tried to get her hair cut before going to Belize. Shannon was missing in action. So Jewel decided to get her hair cut while in Belize. She was walking down Main Street, looking at all the colorful cottages when she spotted a white old house with a sign posted "Beautician, male and female." She was in need of a haircut. There's two men on the porch talking. Jewel stops to introduce herself. She makes an appointment for her cut for the following morning.

The following morning, she arrives at the house looking for Jamal but he wasn't around. She waits, after about 15 minutes he appears.

"Sorry Ma'am for being late, I was out having breakfast with my friend. He's visiting from the states. Give me a minute to set things up."

"Okay."

"I'll be right back."

"Where is he going to cut my hair?" Jewel thought. *"I don't want to go inside his house. Is it safe for me to do that? He does have a great spirit. I can feel it. I'll be fine."*

He yells at Jewel from within the house. "Come on inside. I'm ready!"

She opens the screen door and heads in the direction where she hears Jamal's voice.

She walks into an open space that is set up as a full hair salon. The walls are covered in mirrors. He has a hair washing station, two hair salon chairs where you push your feet to make the chair go up and down.

"Come on over. Have a seat." He wraps a waterproof cloth around her neck and adjusts the chair up and down slightly.

The room was lit from the daylight and you can hear the rusty aluminum fan rattling that was attached to the wall. There were a few spots of maroon paint chipping away on the walls. The place looked like it could have been in a movie scene. Jamal had an old Caribbean salon with a lot of character.

Jamal was born in Belize, but grew up in Brooklyn. The conversation between Jamal and Jewel was very different from the conversation between Shannon and Jewel. Jewel was doing all the talking when Jamal was cutting her hair. Jewel talked so much, she reminded herself of a lonely woman who is super happy to interact with a human. Jamal made her feel so comfortable and relaxed. She was happy to be in his presence. He's a tall slender black man with life experience. Jewel isn't physically attracted to him, she has no desire to jump his bones. She feels safe in his company and could have spent the day with him.

Jamal is an ex military person, so Jewel discussed her brother being in the Army and servicing in the Iraq war. The hardship and toll that Jewel's brother being in the war took on the family, was undeniable. Jamal just listened as Jewel rambled on and on about her life in Lake Avid. The racism she has experienced, and why she continues to live in a place where she is judged by the color of her skin.

Jamal is quiet for the most part, with a yes or no here or there while Jewel keeps yapping away.

She enjoyed traveling alone. Jewel started traveling alone at the age of twenty-four. Her first destination was Nassau, Bahamas. She chose the Bahamas because it was a short flight from JFK. Jewel would party all night. She would hook up with the locals and go bar hopping, take boat rides and she didn't have to pay for anything. The men would take care of the bills. Now with Jewel's age, she doesn't get the same treatment as when she was younger. Jewel now sees it in Jolly. Jolly travels with Jewel usually once a year. The young men treat Jolly the same as Jewel recalls being treated when she was younger traveling throughout the Caribbean.

Jewel has also calmed down with her age. She doesn't go out at night hanging out at the bars as she did when she was younger. She's very aware of not trying to run low on money before her next pay day. Jewel has gone on these trips and her money has gotten low. It has happened more than one time. Jewel travels with cash and tries not to go to the local banks. Bank fees can be high, but if you run out of money you have to be careful not to run out of food.

Every time Jewel travels alone, she hopes to reflect on her life and see what changes she can make to help improve herself as a person. She reflects on her goals of taking care of her mother. Her dreams for her future retirement and what that will look like. In Placencia, it is quiet, not many people around, which makes accomplishing her goal easy.

Jewel spends miles of beach space with about two dozen people. It's a time to be with nature. The yellow sun is blazing over the turquoise gleaming sea. The sand is so hot on Jewel's feet that she quickly puts her flip flops on. The beach has colorful cottages and restaurants lined up for miles. Jewel can hear a little bit of the Caribbean music in the background.

Here in Placencia, anyone can walk down the street and grab a mango off the trees. There is nothing more juicy and sweet than taking a bite into a ripe mango that you picked yourself. Coconut trees are lined up and down the beach. If anyone can reach or grab a coconut off the tree they are welcomed to eat them. The only issue with the coconuts is that they are just so difficult to open. Jewel watched the locals use a machete to get to the coconut juice. New York State is the apple capital, yet when people walk down the street there are no apple trees lined up to pick from.

The Belizeans are such hardworking people. Working long hours, this one local lady said she left home at 4:30 a.m. to get to Placencia at 7:30 a.m. She was selling little handmade baskets. The Mexican Belizean's food Jewel has been enjoying is open from 6:30 a.m. to 9:30 p.m. with an elderly lady cooking in a hot truck. The people are resilient, strong, and humble.

Jewel has experienced discrimination two times since she has been in Belize, of course from the usual Jewish and American people. Jewel is hanging out at the beach. It is very quiet until this one lady shows up with her family. She was speaking Hebrew and English, so Jewel knew she was Jewish. The lady was so loud, demanding that the man she was with take pictures of her. Due to how loud she was, Jewel was looking at her. Usually when people are loud like that they want attention. When the man finally took the picture the family sat in the restaurant chairs behind where Jewel was sitting on the beach. The lady was still being loud so Jewel could hear everything she was saying. Another lady approaches the beach and, although Jewel can't see the lady, she can hear the Jewish lady's loud voice. The Jewish lady complimented the lady on a flower she had in her hair.

"That flower is the reason you have a man standing by your side."

The Jewish lady was trying to shame Jewel. What's wrong with traveling alone? Nothing. People have a fear of traveling alone. Jewel gets it; traveling alone isn't for everyone. Jolly most likely would not jump on a plane just to hang out on a beach all day doing nothing alone. Jolly would hop on a plane with an agenda. But what's up with the idea that a man is required for everything? Should women just stop living because they don't have a man? A man is not required to be alive. Jewel hopes all women have enough confidence within themselves to stand alone, even if they feel lonely. Traveling alone helps Jewel become stronger and more resilient as the culture of the people she visits.

Everyone should like themselves enough to look in the mirror everyday. While you're looking in that mirror ask yourself if you are happy with who you are and if not, how can you make a change to be a better you. Take baby steps each day to improve who you are, become a person happy to look in the mirror everyday.

Jewel looks in the mirror to admire her body, her beauty, her hair. Jewel touches her body, her breast, her lips, her vagina, and so on. We all should look in that mirror and be comfortable with what we see and if you're not happy with what you see, make a change. The main reason people refuse to make a change in their life when they are not happy about something they see in the mirror is usually from being lazy. Laziness is the true mental disease in the world.

On Jewel's second day at her Airbnb, a white American couple is hanging out in front of their unit. After being out at the beach for a few hours, Jewel arrives back at her Airbnb.

"Someone is staying in that apartment," the man yells as Jewel approaches her door.

"Yes, it's me," Jewel replies. It's an Airbnb for goodness sake. There's no signs posted when people check in or check out. Once Jewel entered her key into the door, the man says to his wife, "Oh, I guess it is hers." Jewel could have looked at this in a couple ways. He's just a nosy Airbnb guest or he doesn't expect to see a black woman as his next door neighbor while he is on vacation.

Jewel looks like she is from the Caribbean with her soft, beautiful coco skin. The only way a person knows she's an American is when she opens her mouth to talk. He was an American, so Jewel knew for sure it's the fact that she was a black woman going into the apartment. He thought Jewel was a local.

Truth be told, black people have a keen sense of when there is a racist person in their presence. Jewel has been in that position, especially at work. She could recall when she knew in her heart that there was a racist woman at her front desk counter to check in at the hotel. Her attitude was above entitlement. *OMG, why is there a black woman checking me in?* It's sad when you see another woman behaving this way because of another woman's beauty. Think about it! What is racism actually about? Isn't it really the same meaning as jealousy? That is the real definition of what racism is, being jealous of another race.

Jewel recalls Jamal saying all races have their problems and he was so right. The hardest truth of Jamal's statement is the black on black crime. Black men killing black men is the saddest heartbreak of all time. The killing is out of jealousy as well. This is an era where black people are becoming billionaires. Jewel is aware that in her lifetime she gets to witness rich black men and women, and so many people are hating that within their own race. It hurts that black people can be so divided because of jealousy.

Jewel can see the jealousy, but it's not the fault of God making some people more successful than others. Jewel believes God has a different journey for each person to reach their greatest success. To get to that success, patience, belief, fear and vulnerability are required. These qualities are extremely difficult to have all at once. To see a black man on the rise accomplishing his dreams while another black man is failing causes extreme jealousy. The jealous person doesn't understand being patient and waiting on God. It's also sad when black people are not supportive of each other. Look at the Asian community for example.

Each place that Jewel travels has a Chinese family that owns a supermarket. The Chinese are successful no matter where in the world they live because they stick together. They take care of each other. There is no envy when it comes to their own. The Black community could learn a lot from Asian culture.

Even though traveling alone can be lonely sometimes, Belize was one of Jewel's favorite solo trips. This trip made a change for Jewel; she decided to stop smoking weed. The weed smoking was taking a toll on her lungs. That's what looking in the mirror did for Jewel while on this trip. Edibles it will be.

So after check out, Jewel leaves a nice review for her host and they in turn left a nice review for Jewel.

"Jewel was a lovely guest and a pleasure to host. She was quiet, friendly, and left the apartment very clean. We would certainly recommend her to other hosts."

This is the behavior you would hope people have while traveling. Hands down the best thing about Belize is the people. The people are kind. Thank you, Belize! Time to make that long trip back home to Lake Avid.

WINTER

Hockey

The game called "hockey" arrived in the United States in the nineteenth century. The first hockey team in Lake Avid was organized for boys in 1901. However, it was more popular in Canada until the teams started traveling to the northern states to compete in the Collegiate Tournaments. The games were played with two teams of six members each; one goalie, two defensemen, and three wingers. Although the equipment then was skates and gloves and little protection, rules and regulations now insist they wear skates, wool stockings (held up by garter belts), knee pads, hip pads, cup, elbow pads, shoulder pads, neck braces, gloves, and helmet (including a mouth guard). All under shorts held up by suspenders and a heavy jersey blazoned with the team's logo. The object of the games is to hit a three inch black "puck" down the ice with a curved stick, past the goalie and into the net to score. Skating skills are a necessity as well as agility. The game is kept in control with a Referee and a Linesman who call all the penalties such as elbowing, off sides, etc. There is no age limit, kids start as young as four and continue into at least their fifties.

Hockey has been a prominent draw in Lake Avid. The early years brought many teams to the area for weekend competitions. Before the construction of the Olympic Arena, hockey games were held on Mirror Lake. There were hockey boxes erected in the middle of the lake with the other skaters staying on the outside in the oval. The

Lake Avid Club constructed several hockey boxes in the area known as their tennis courts. The snow was cleared with horses and a wooden plow and then watered down to make the smooth surfaces for the skaters. College Weeks were known to bring in hundreds of students and their families for rigorous competitions. An area in front of the high school was also flooded for local team exhibitions.

In the late 1940s, a group of locals started an organization called: The Lake Avid Pee Wee Association which was established for the youth of the community. Thereafter, every winter weekend was full of hockey games, speed skating meets, etc. The climax of the year was completed with The International Tournament. Teams across the US and Canada met from Thursday to Sunday in hockey games for all ages. One year, there were 72 teams competing. This tournament is still active and in 2011 there were fifty-nine teams from New York, New Jersey, and Massachusetts with five teams from Lake Avid competing.

The Roamers, a semi-pro hockey team, was organized in 1946. At that time the team was mostly Canadians, however, during the next ten or more years, local young men joined the team and the Lake Avid community had the opportunity to enjoy hockey every weekend at the Olympic Arena.

The highlight of hockey in Lake Avid is the Miracle on Ice during the 1980 Olympics. The Olympic team was made up of various college men pulled together by a dedicated coach to form a tight, fast skating, correct passing, and medal hungry team. When faced with the older, more talented, more experienced Russian team as the underdogs, they were ready to prove everyone wrong and come out of the fray with a win. To the fans cheering, "USA" and the announcer hollering, "Do you believe in miracles?" They did just that with one of the most exciting hockey games of the century. However, the medal wasn't in their hands yet. They had to beat the Finn's to achieve the coveted Gold Medal. Again they proved what an awesome team they were and battled their way to a 4-2 win. It was an Olympic experience that will be talked about in the hockey families for years to come.

There are lots of opportunities for hockey around town. One venue is the relatively new Hockey Box located on the Southeast corner of the Olympic Speed skating Oval property. Entry is free and rules are posted. This rink is refrigerated and was donated by Ironman USA to the people of Lake Avid. The North Elba Park District plows a couple of skating areas on Mirror Lake, one of them being at the Lake Avid Public Beach. There are hockey nets there that are free to use. Sometimes when there is little or no snow on top of the ice, one can skate from one end of the lake to the other. Pick-up hockey games can be seen all over the place. There are also several ponds along the hiking trails where one can see locals playing a game of hockey on occasion.

Pond Hockey is becoming a popular organized sport around North America lately. In fact, Lake Avid and Can/Am Hockey sponsor an annual Pond Hockey Tournament in mid-January every year. Ten hockey rinks are cleared on Mirror Lake and a round robin tournament elapses over the course of the weekend.

On the inside rinks, hockey games are plentiful in the winter season. The Pee Wee program sponsors games regularly, as do the local high schools. Both Can/Am Hockey and Canadian Hockey Enterprises hold tournaments on most weekends in the fall through spring seasons."
—*Bev Reid, North Elba Town Historian*

https://www.lakeplacid.com/do/outdoors/winterspring/hockey

The Garden Tree Lakeside Resort and all the other hotels in the area depend on hockey events to keep them afloat for the fall and winter seasons. It's big money; families spending thousands upon thousands of dollars to have their child or children participate in the sport of hockey.

Brenda and Jewel are working this evening and the phone rings. Brenda answers. She completes the call and hangs up.

It doesn't happen that often, but Brenda is looking serious. She's not laughing.

"Someone called and said that someone took a shit on the fourth floor," Brenda reports. "I'll be right back."

"What? Okay."

She starts walking in the south direction, takes the steps up to the loft area, and she continues walking. Quickly, she returns to the front desk with a frown on her face.

"I can't believe one of these little fuckers took a shit on the carpet floor! I'm not picking that shit up."

"No way!" exclaims Jewel.

"Yes, one of the guests told me a little boy did it. Let me go check the cameras."

They walk into Karen and Ginger's office to check the camera. Lo and behold, there's a little blond boy shitting in the hallway. He looks around the age of seven or eight years old.

"Ew, that's so nasty!" They yell in unison.

They both leave the office but Jewel walks back to the front desk. Brenda grabs a cloth out of the bathroom. She heads back in the south direction and decides to put the cloth over the shit. She then walks back down to the front desk and radios a houseman to clean it up.

Brenda's shift report this evening:

Electrum showed up around 3:12 p.m. to check out the situation with room 101. They could not fix the issue and there was no follow-up.

Some of the little guys used the sled. All were returned.

A little blond boy is seen on camera taking a shit on the fourth floor hallway. That's where I draw the line; Shawn cleaned the mess up.

Houseman Joe stayed until 7:00 p.m. He salted and plowed the hill.

#167: The fireplace is not working, there is no pilot light that we can see. Shawn took the battery out of the fireplace because it was beeping and it smelled like gas a bit.

A lot of people were in the lobby, drinking and hanging out all night since their television didn't work.

Lots of entitled people not wanting to clean up after themselves, many bottles and cans picked up. The recycling for Amanda (housekeeper) is in the back room.

A dog had diarrhea in the lobby, Shawn cleaned it up.

The children stuffed the vending machine on the second floor with paper and it's out of order.

Several cap guns have been collected.

The pool has alcoholic cans and bottles. Sorry no one will listen. Pool closed at 9:10 p.m.

Adam came around 8:30 p.m. to check some rooms and check on us!

Almost out of wine glasses upstairs/Can someone please restock in the morning?

9:10 p.m. lobby full of people eating and drinking after I put up signs. Had to remove couch (in front of the television) cushions, pillows, and blankets because they spilled blue slushy all over them.

Kids are breaking other teams' hockey sticks and trashing them. Children walking around crying, parents arguing with a rival team then the parents started fighting with each other in the lobby.

Tanner did what he could to control the situation.

Milkshake spilled on carpet on 3 south.

The shoe in the lost and found basket that is missing is from a child taunting the adult in room #122 and this guest chased him and got his shoe only. Please take the room number when returning.

The next day...

Karen finds out about the hockey boy shitting on the hotel carpet and she blacklisted the entire hockey team from being able to stay at the hotel. The front desk feels violated after being so disrespected in their workplace.

The word spreads throughout the hotel that a little boy shitted on the hallway carpet. One parent was in disbelief and accused a pet of doing it but it was recorded on camera. The parents were embarrassed and ashamed of the behavior of the kids in the hotel.

Entitled people, yes, I'm talking to you, you do realize how it looks to the world? It looks as if you forgot to teach your children basic manners, like saying, "Please and thank you." Instead, the kids are telling hotel staff that their parents told them they don't have to answer to the "Help." Entitled adults are raising a bunch of jerks and assholes. To raise your child or children to believe they're too good of a human to have basic simple manners is sad and rude.

The part of the country where you live is how the front desk staff knows what type of child or children they will have to babysit. Children from Long Island and parts of New Jersey are the most entitled, biggest jerks and assholes that come to the resort. These children are blinded by entitlement and it's scary.

It's normal practice, in the hockey world, to leave young children wandering around the hotel alone while mommy and daddy are at the bar. It's nice that the hotel offers trivia quizzes. It allows kids to wander around the hotel, making discoveries. Jewel could only imagine the little blond boy, probably couldn't find his family, maybe it's the reason he took a shit on the floor.

Jewel remembers Madeleine McCann. Jewel found it unusual for parents to leave their very young children alone. She thinks about her every time she sees a two or three year old child wandering around the hotel lobby alone, it's sad.

The following evening...

Elizabeth and Jewel are working together, once again they're without a houseman. Jewel doesn't mind taking guest extra towels, shampoo/conditioner, and toilet tissue. She has no interest and will not respond to a code four or anything to do with bodily fluids. A code four is when the toilet is backed up.

The phone rings. Elizabeth answers. A guest on the fourth floor called. "My son got sick and threw up in the hallway. Can you please have someone come clean it up?"

Elizabeth is fuming.

"I wasn't hired for this shit. Karen refuses to give me a supervisor title and a raise. Yet, I have to clean up vomit. We never have a houseman on duty..."

Multiple calls come into the front desk about the smell on the fourth floor. Elizabeth is moving along slowly. She threatens to walk out and never return.

"Back in the day," Jewel thought. *"The Black person would have easily been assigned to clean up that mess. Times have changed and this black woman hasn't cleaned up another person's throw up yet."*

Jewel is reminded of a time she traveled alone to Boston for a night. She had a desire for lobster. A quick hour flight for lobster was worth it to her. She booked a hotel room. After dinnertime, she headed to the hotel bar and had a drink. After one drink, she decided to walk across the street to the liquor store. Jewel purchased herself a bottle of Cabernet Sauvignon. She headed back to the hotel and spent a lonely night drinking and watching television. Jewel was wasted! She fell asleep. Around 2:00 a.m. her body woke her up and she threw up, right there on the floor next to the bed. Piles upon piles of throw up ended up on the floor.

Not once did it occur to her to pick up the phone. Dial 0. And say, "Hey, I had a drunken night, can you please send housekeeping up?"

Well, in this case, according to Elizabeth. She goes up to the reported throw up, and upon arrival, several guests are standing around waiting. She assumed to point out where the smell was coming from. Jewel is sure Elizabeth's nose would have discovered where the smell was coming from.

However, in this case, the people were hecklers. "Ew that nasty, you have to clean that up? I would never..." Elizabeth comes marching down the step from the loft area. From her mannerisms, Jewel can tell she's super pissed. She's walking quickly and there's a frown on her face.

"Jewel, I can't take this anymore. I feel undervalued working in this hotel."

She was practically in tears.

"Those little boys were shooting little spit balls at me, calling me a fat bitch while I was cleaning up."

"WOW! What? Are you serious? I'm so sorry, Elizabeth. I don't understand these children, behaving like this."

"When I was hired, I was not told I had to clean up bodily fluids. Karen treats me like a stepchild. I'm over this place."

"Elizabeth, go speak with Karen about what's going on before you do anything dramatic."

"Yeah, I'm going to have to speak with her tomorrow. She is going to have to hire a housekeeper for the evening shift. I'm only going to do the job I was hired for."

"Thank you. Elizabeth, please don't leave."

"Thank you for listening to me, Jewel."

"Of course, Elizabeth, that's what I'm here for, to keep you from jumping off the ledge."

They both have a quick laugh and then the ladies continue to work in silence.

Ronnie arrives for his shift and the ladies head out for the evening.

Winter

Winter is the second busiest season in Lake Avid. The crystal snow is falling with children running around having snowball fights and making snow angels. The weekends are bustling with skiers, bobsledders, ice skaters, and of course, hockey players. The Christmas lights are strung around the street light poles on the mile long Main Street. The laughter of children skipping on the granite sidewalk brings a joyful spirit to the community.

Mirror Lake is frozen, and with the dog sledders preparing for the season, there's excitement in the air with laughter and smiling faces. The long lines for the Mirror Lake toboggan shoot run up to Main Street. People are strolling around drinking hot chocolate and apple cider.

Families and their dogs keep the colorful shops on Main Street busy. Along the Main Street are several restaurants, a Starbucks, a few real estate offices, several hotels, souvenirs shops, a candy store, a chocolate factory, plus so much more.

Wintertime has the best quality of air. Jewel breathes as much fresh winter air into her lungs as she can. The temperatures can be brutally negative, 25 degrees is expected every year, along with average snowfalls of 100 inches.

Lake Avid is not a place to live if you cannot withstand those types of temperatures. It is the reason why the population is low and there aren't many Black families in the community. Black families are known to live in warmer climates. The word around the community is most people move away from the area after their third winter. The very expensive houses along Mirror Lake are empty in the wintertime. It's a wealthy community and Lake Avid is the place the rich buy their second homes.

Homes are also being used as Airbnbs. The real estate businesses on Main Street manage the properties while the families are away. Lots of money flows through the area because of all the sports venues within Lake Avid and the surrounding area. You'll meet the most physically fit, focus minded, energized humans in the world in Lake Avid. There's amazing sportsmanship in the air. The athletes compete with good spirits. They take pride in their hard work and they know how to celebrate success. It's one of the reasons why Jewel moved to Lake Avid. Lake Avid offers a whole package of wealth in the heart and the spirit of sportsmanship.

The vibe is very relaxed and mellow in Lake Avid. The place has changed Jewel. When she first arrived in Lake Avid, she was stressed out all the time. It was her nature from living in NYC to be stressed. The lifestyles are so different, Jewel changed with her new environment. A change for the better, a change of increased self-love and self-growth. Jewel is more relaxed with an improved attitude.

Elizabeth and Jewel are working this evening. As soon as

they arrive at work, people are gossiping. Oh my! Brenda,
has given in her two-week notice. Jewel is happy for
Brenda. At the same time, she's having mixed emotions.
She doesn't want to work with a bunch of "Karens,"
without Brenda. Brenda is much better at dealing with
them than she is. Jewel isn't as patient as Brenda. She's
only interested in working. She could lose her temper
dealing with a "Karen."

Elizabeth and Jewel's shift is quiet for the most part.
They're sitting around talking about what's going on with
Brenda. Jewel is wondering why Brenda didn't tell her that
she found new employment. While they're talking,
Elizabeth notices people hanging out in the loft area.

"Jewel, let's keep an eye on the group in the loft, it looks
like they may be drinking."

A few hours pass by and the voices in the loft are getting
louder.

It's a Russian group of four men who have been drinking
vodka all evening. Jewel and Elizabeth haven't said
anything since the group isn't bothering anyone, but their
voices are getting louder as the evening goes along.

At 10:00 p.m., the lobby is settling down for the evening
and now the Russians are rowdy.
Elizabeth walks up the stairs to the loft and lets the guests
know that it's quiet time in the lobby. She asked that they
keep the noise level down and/or go to their rooms. One of
the men stands up and heads in the directions of the hotel's
rooms. Elizabeth returns to her station.

Five minutes later...

The Russian man returns with a karaoke machine and starts a political rant. "This is not a communist country. I can say what I want and when I want."

Shawn is radioed and arrives at the front desk shortly after. Elizabeth asks him to please speak with the Russians before she calls the cops.

Shawn agrees. He goes up to the loft to speak with the Russians. Words go back and forth between Shawn and one of the men. Elizabeth and Jewel are behind the front desk counter, they can see the Russian man is pointing his finger into Shawn's chest with his voice escalating for the ladies to hear him. The Russian man is screaming, "Isn't this a free country?" He continues pushing his finger into Shawn's chest saying, "Hum? Hum? Now why don't you go do something like collect the trash."

"You're a loser!" Shawn screams to the man. He walks away and heads down the steps towards the front desk.

"Elizabeth, you're going to have to call 911. These people are overly excited to be in a free country."

The police are called to the hotel. Karen is also called. Karen wants the cops to escort the Russians to their rooms. The police do as wished. The police leave and Shawn leaves.

Due to the previous conflict between Shawn and Ronnie, Karen has instructed Shawn to leave 15 minutes early and

Ronnie to arrive 15 minutes later. This way, they will not run into one another.

Ronnie has arrived for his shift. The Russian man, the one who had the karaoke machine, approaches him. He tells Ronnie that a White, long, bearded man was cursing and yelling at him. This is just the fuel Ronnie has been waiting for. His sweet revenge. Shawn still locks the Devine mall door every night.

Ronnie's shift report for this evening reads as follows:

- *Guests came to complain. These guests are disruptive, sure, but they didn't come to complain about being kicked out of the lobby or turning their music off this time. They said Shawn ("the man with the huge beard") was using derogatory language against them as they argued. I'm not sure how Shawn gets away with a complete lack of manners in conflict. He calls his co-workers (at least me) mean things as well. We use polite language when dealing with guests no matter what.*

- *Phones and internet died at about 3 A.M. Nothing unusual.*

Jewel had the next day off. So, Elizabeth texted Jewel later that day.

"Hey Jewel, I hope you're enjoying your day off but I couldn't wait to update you on the latest drama. Ronnie wrote about what happened with the Russians in his shift report last night. The new girl that was just hired, who's

training to replace Brenda, showed Shawn the email.
Shawn called Ronnie a baby and a punk. This did not go
well for the new girl either. Karen yelled at her for
showing Shawn the email in the first place. Karen asked
her why in her right mind would she show Shawn that
email? Shawn said he was done with the drama. He
dropped his keys and walked out the building."

Jewel is picking clothes up off her bedroom floor when she
hears her phone ping. Her phone is charging, while laying
on her bed. She picks the phone up and sees a message
from Elizabeth. She reads the message with surprise of
what Elizabeth is reporting to her. Jewel replied, "OMG,
Elizabeth, that's a lot of drama at work today."

"I know! You should be happy you have the day off. I
hope you're enjoying yourself."

Jewel types her reply. "Yes, I'm relaxing and doing a little
cleaning around the house. BUT Elizabeth did you hear the
exciting news? Mary had a baby girl on December 15. She
named her Ryan. She weighed 6lbs 9oz and she's 20 inches
tall."

"Yes, I heard." Elizabeth replies. "Karen went around the
hotel announcing it to everyone. I am so happy for Mary.
I'm going to have to go to the store and buy her a baby gift.
Jewel, I have to go there's a line."

Jewel types. "Okay, see you tomorrow. Enjoy the rest of
your day at work."

Shawn was never to be seen again. Ronnie is over the

moon with excitement. The next evening, Ronnie doesn't walk through the hotel lobby for work. He walks through the Devine mall. As the saying goes, "payback is a bitch."

The next night ...

Elizabeth and Jewel are working. Hockey is in the house. Due to how disruptive and destructive the kids are, security is a must in the hotel. Tanner, Brenda's boyfriend, is working security this evening.

It's 10:30 p.m. and the phone rings. Elizabeth answers. "I'll take care of it, ma'am." She hangs up the phone.

Elizabeth walks toward the door to exit the front desk space. "That was a noise complaint," she says to Jewel. "There are people on the beach being very loud."

Jewel follows Elizabeth to the window. They confirm there is a loud group on the beach and then walk back to their stations. Elizabeth radioes Tanner to the front desk. Once he has arrived, she directs him to the complaint. Tanner heads downstairs to the beach area to deal with the rowdy people. He comes back to the front desk and has snow covering parts of his body.

"Two men started throwing snowballs at me," he cries. He drops his keys on the front desk counter. "This is not the job for me." Tanner heads to the door to walk out.

Ronnie appears right before Tanner is out the door and stops him.

"What's going on?" Ronnie asks.

"Some rowdy group threw snowballs at him," Elizabeth explains.

"Oh, let me handle this." Ronnie marches down to the beach area. Elizabeth, Tanner, and Jewel have to watch this, so they walk over to the window. They see men and children all throwing snowballs at Ronnie. He rushes back upstairs and calls the police. The police arrive and break up the party. One of the men came up to the lobby.

"How could you call the police on us?"

"Sir, the hotel has a 10:00 p.m. curfew that you disrespected. We have to be mindful of all the guests staying in the hotel. People have the right to a peaceful night's sleep. There are occupied rooms on the beach. The noise carries into the guest's room," Elizabeth explains.

Now that Ronnie has settled into the evening and the police are gone, Elizabeth and Jewel clock out for the night. They walk out together. Jewel heads home. Tanner is never seen at the hotel again.

The next day, Karen calls Jewel early and asks if she can work some extra hours in the laundry department before her shift begins at 3:00 p.m. Jewel agrees to come in at noon.

The next afternoon, Jewel arrives in the laundry department. Upon her arrival she is not alone, there's a blonde lady with glasses folding sheets.

Chandler and Jack have the day off.

"Hi, I'm Jewel."

"Hi, I'm Helen. Chandler told me to expect you. I was just hired for the overnight shifts."

"That's great! They really do need help as I guess you can see."

Jewel looks towards the dirty clothes laundry bins. Both ladies look at each other with a grin.

"Yes, I am training during the day for the next two weeks."

"I see why Karen asked me to come in," Jewel thought. *"There's a new person working alone."*

Helen is a twenty-eight year old, middle height, overweight, mother of three young girls. Jewel thought Helen looked very tired. Jewel noticed Helen has a stench. The word around the hotel is she's homeless, living in her car. Housekeeping reports she fell on hard times. Her three daughters were taken by the state of NY due to a meth problem within the family's household.

The weather is getting worse as the days go by. Helen comes into the hotel and asked the front desk staff if she can rent a room for the night. Her stay in her car is becoming more and more difficult.

Rules have changed at the resort. Several housekeepers, and/or houseman, will come to the front desk, crying a sad story in hopes of getting a Specialty suite at a discounted rate. That way, they can have sex in style for the night. Elizabeth is gullible. Staff members will come to her station crying. *They broke up with their boyfriend/ girlfriend and had too much to drink and needed a room for the night.* What's really happening is there was no fight, they want Elizabeth to feel sad, and it works.

It happens so often that Karen changed the rules for staff members who wanted a room in the hotel. First, the person must receive approval two weeks in advance from management. Second, the staff cannot stay during a holiday weekend.

Come to find out Ellen, Head of Housekeeping, is how Helen got the laundry attendance position. She knew her friend. Ellen knew Helen needed a job, so she spoke with Becky and she hired her. Ellen was also aware Helen was living in her car.

The first night, Helen came to the front desk for a room. Ginger was working and Jewel got approval for her to stay the night. The second night she came back, Ginger said no. Ginger expressed that she couldn't live in the hotel and that she couldn't afford to either. Even, discounted to $50.00 a night, that added up to $1,500.00 per month. Ellen was asked if she knew Helen was living in her car? She didn't want to get involved.

Well, Elizabeth became very concerned about Helen sleeping in her car. She called Karen and told her what was going on. Karen told her she can stay in the hotel, at no cost, until they could find a more permanent solution.

Karen quickly got Helen into permanent housing. Helen starts to get her life in order. Helen and her boyfriend move into the same building as Ronnie aka "Killer."

Reviews

T he resort reviews are very important. Reviews can make or break a business. Karen takes reviews very seriously. When a staff member's name is mentioned in a positive review, an additional $10.00 is added to his or her paycheck. An incentive to be the best they can be. The second shift reviews are outstanding:

Jewel is a gem!

Elizabeth's HOMEMADE hot chocolate chip cookies every night were AMAZING!

Brenda had the sweetest smile. She was always laughing.

Elizabeth upgraded my family to a Specialty suite, it worked out better for our family.

Jewel provided excellent customer service and went out of her way to make us feel at home. She deserves a bonus. Her passion for excellent service was obvious.

Our fireplace in our room didn't work, having a fireplace was the reason we reserved this room. We called the front desk for assistance. Someone came to help, but unsuccessfully. I was very upset. I called the front desk again and this time I got Brenda on the line. She suggested that we move to the same room, two floors up, (a better view). My husband and I spoke about it and we decided to move. Brenda gave us a complimentary bottle of white wine, and the fireplace was lit when we arrived to our new room. Brenda apologized for us having to make the move. She made us feel welcomed and comfortable. Excellent customer service.

Relaxing Vacation! From Samantha making sure I had the perfect room, Becky picking me up from the train station, houseman Joe's beautiful holiday lights. Elizabeth and Jewel made us "feel at home." Gilligan, Stella, and Mary helped us navigate our stay-I definitely plan to come back.

A very pleasant week, we recently spent a week at The Garden Tree Lakeside Resort and could not have been happier. Everyone on the staff we interacted with was delightful. Jewel, Elizabeth, and Gilligan at the front desk were always pleasant and fun to talk to whenever we passed through the lobby. Housekeeping staff members always greeted us and asked if we needed help. Thank you to all the staff at the Garden Tree.

The location and facilities are great, and having on-site, underground parking during a 1-inch snowfall was a super bonus. The hotel connection to the Garden of Eden and the Spa Garden of Flower is very nice. There are many generous choices with more nice staff members.

We stayed at the Garden Tree Lakeside Resort 15 years ago, and when we wanted to spend a week enjoying the town's Christmas decorations and events, we returned to the Garden Tree. Being 15 years older, The Garden Tree looks 15 years newer, and is the only hotel in Lake Avid we would ever consider visiting in the area. Thank you to all for making our stay as nice as could be.

Karen or the marketing manager, Judy, replies to every review.

Brenda, Elizabeth, and Jewel are appreciative of the extra $10.00. The reviews show Karen that they have respect and take pride in their work. Of course, if the staff looks good, management looks good, too. The author of *Dear Entitled Hotel Guests,* will be affected by the reviews, too. The better the reviews are for the book, the better the sales will be. Thank you, readers, in advance for all the positive reviews.

It's a couple days before Brenda's final departure from the hotel. It's the last evening, Elizabeth, Brenda, and Jewel will be working together. Brenda and Elizabeth are working the front desk while Jewel is working the credential table.

The credentials are given to all the hockey athletes and their family members. The credentials allow access to meals served at the Garden of Eden and some events at the Sports Center. For example, admission into the museum.

On this day, Karen calls Jewel into her office.

In the past, Karen has called Jewel into her office on one other occasion. In that case, Jewel didn't charge enough for a room. A couple approached Jewel's station. They wanted to surprise their parents for her mom's birthday. They paid for a room the parents reserved.

"Why didn't you charge the correct amount?" Karen looked Jewel in the eye and asked.

Jewel remembered writing notes in the parents' profile via Hotel Master.

"It was a birthday surprise," Jewel said, confused. "I do remember that." Jewel had no explanation for why she didn't charge enough. "Did Hotel Master change the rack rate after the bill was paid?" Jewel asked.

"Well, I don't know, that's a good question. Let me check."

Karen logged into Hotel Master. "No, that didn't happen. Let me show you the correct way, so this error doesn't happen again."

"Okay."

Karen showed Jewel a technique on Hotel Master to make sure the error didn't happen again. Jewel returned to her station.

Today, the vibe was different. Karen looked serious as Jewel entered the office.

"I want to talk with you, please have a seat."

"What could this be about?" Jewel thought. She is a great employee. If Karen asks something of Jewel; she does it. She works overtime. ALL holidays including Thanksgiving and she's scheduled to work Christmas Day, too. She's assigned to work New Year's Eve as well. Jewel is Karen's

"Yes" lady.

"Jewel, can you please work the next two nights? Brenda called out...Jewel, can you please work the overnight shift? Ronnie, can't make it. He's sick...Jewel, extra hands are needed in laundry, can you please put in a few extra hours?" Every time, Jewel replies, "YES!"

Karen shows appreciation. She would slide Jewel a $50.00 here and there, one of those $50's was presented with a note:

Jewel, I just wanted to thank you for covering the last 2 nights. I know it was last minute and I just want you to know I really appreciate it and appreciate you. Thank you for being a part of our team. Love, K

She thought it was the sweetest note she ever received from a boss. She started researching Amazon for a nice Christmas gift to give Karen. She found a German made pen and thought it would have been a perfect gift. Well, that all was about to change and quickly.

Truth is Karen didn't have to ask Jewel to work extra hours. Jewel would see the need in the hotel and offer to help. As long as Jewel was getting paid time plus time and a half, she would work. But, the company doesn't pay time and a half when you work on a holiday. Something that was upsetting to staff.

"*Oh boy,*" Jewel wondered. "*Do they have me on camera purchasing weed from housekeeping?*"

"What's up?" Jewel asks.

"A few of your co-workers have come to me and told me you're cold."

"What? I'm here to work, they don't have to like me."

Jewel is surprised! She thought she got along well with mostly everyone. At least everyone on the second shift. The second shift doesn't really get to spend much time with most of the other staff. That shift is gone by 4:00 p.m.

Karen is sitting on top of her desk, looking down on Jewel. She hops off her desk, walks over to the table, grabs a piece of paper, and hands it over to her.

It's a review, it reads as follows:

My partner and I enjoyed our vacation. I'm giving the resort four stars. The hot tub was super hot. I went to the front desk to report the problem to the clerk. She informed me there were no housemen on duty. And she's the only person working on the shift. I was surprised when she said, "Don't get in the hot..."

Jewel put down the paper on the table and said, "Okay. I do remember that lady coming to the desk about the hot tub. A different guest came the next evening with the same complaint. I wrote it in my shift report both nights."

Karen says, "Yeah, not fixing the hot tub after the first complaint was our fault. I'm not here to talk about that. I don't want you telling people to not get into the hot tub."

"Is this really a big deal that I told someone not to get in a hot tub? Because it was too hot and you know some people don't think."

"Yes, I don't want you telling people that."

"Okay. This is nonsense, where's the positive reviews? That's what you should be bringing me in here for."

Karen is surprised by Jewel's remarks.

"We pay you $10.00 for each positive review."

"Okay, but when I see you, don't I say hi?"

Karen puts both of her hands on her chest and says, "Yes, but it's me!"

Jewel points her hand up and down while speaking. "I treat everyone the same. I don't care how high up you are or if you're in housekeeping. I don't treat certain groups of people better than others."

This is the moment Jewel knew Karen was a racist. Karen feels she's better than certain groups of people because she's White and rich, which equals entitled. In reality, she's mad because she knows the truth about herself. She's not special. She was born a rich, White woman. That doesn't make you special without good character.

"Do you have problems with anyone?" Karen asks.

"Well, I don't really care for Gilligan. I think he's a rat."

"What do you mean?" Karen asks.

"He gathers information, negative information, and runs in here and reports back to you. I don't like those kinds of people."

"He's not like that."

"Okay, if you say so."

In the middle of the conversation, Jewel recalls something. Now, she knows what this is about. The two young White racist women that work in the hotel. As soon as Jewel realizes a person is racist, she distances herself from them. Jewel doesn't like racist people.

The marketing manager, Judy, is a typical White American "princess." She will only speak to a Black person if she is spoken to first. Brenda and Jewel both noticed it. She ran and told Karen, Jewel was cold because Jewel doesn't speak to her.

It's true. Once Jewel noticed that Judy would only speak with her if she was spoken to first, she stopped speaking to her. If Jewel did not want to speak with someone, she wouldn't. It's her right. Just like it's Judy's right not to speak with a Black person if she doesn't want to. She surely didn't feel the need to go cry to Karen. Jewel didn't care. If you don't want to speak with Jewel because of the color of her skin, fuck you! Of course, the game is to weed the Black people out of the hotel. And it works out for Judy.

Next, the Reservation Manager, Samantha, saw Jewel in the hallway once. Jewel was at the end of a 60-hour work week. So, Jewel was moving along quickly and didn't say hi. Jewel was in her zone, not thinking it was law to speak to every single person she ran into. Samantha's feelings were hurt. She ran and told Karen that Jewel was cold to her. But, she didn't speak to Jewel either while passing by her in the hallway. Jewel is from NYC, not speaking to a person is not a priority in her head. In NYC it's actually normal practice not to speak to everyone. It's not being rude, there are just too many people to speak to.

Both of these women work the day shift. So, Jewel rarely sees them. BUT if she does; she has to stop and kiss their ass? Jewel is too real for these people. Karen encourages people to be fake. It's how she deals with the public. Jewel doesn't kiss ass enough and those two managers are a part of Karen's clique. Whereas, Jewel doesn't give two shits about being part of the "It" group. Jewel wants the money; she is there to work.

Jewel randomly thinks of a time in her 40's that her Black American male manager at a real estate firm called her a crackhead. Jewel is a strong character, she's not into kissing anyone's ass. Life is full of attention seekers. People are not comfortable in their own skin so they look for others to give them that comfort. It's sad, because that means the world is full of a bunch of weak minded people. Pay attention to your own self, have self-love, stop crying for others to notice you.

She should have just called her an *Angry Black Woman*. It's the same thing. Karen is doing too much, calling Jewel into her office with this bullshit.

When someone belittles you, that person is insecure. Belittling someone else makes them feel powerful. Jewel has no interest in giving a bunch of Karen's any power over her. She is there to work, not kiss ass. Once again, this is about the envy of a Black woman. She's too beautiful, too kind hearted, her swag is too tight, her skin is too soft. For Karen to feel better about her insecurities, she drags Jewel into the office about some bullshit. She sits on top of her desk to look down on Jewel versus her sitting in a chair and looking eye level with her.

Racist people freak Jewel out, they're evil people at the end of day. As soon as Jewel realizes a person is racist she gets far far away. Jewel knows at that moment that Karen is racist. She is not going to continue working for a person with such evil in her heart.

Jewel gets up and heads to the door.

"Jewel, can you be nicer?" Karen asks.

Jewel apologizes for taking up so much of Karen's time. She knows she will be giving her notice soon.

Brenda and Elizabeth both exclaim. "What? No way!"

Brenda gives Jewel the Black girl side eye with her lips in a twist. Softly laughing, Brenda chimes in. "You must have offended that Alpha female. You better start kissing these White women's asses. See, that's why I'm out of here. I don't have time to be dealing with a bunch of KARENS."

"You know that's not going to happen. I don't mind working hard. But, I draw the line at kissing these bitches' ass. It's time to start looking for a new job," Jewel replies.

"I don't blame you, something is wrong here. You're the best employee. You do whatever Karen asks of you. She's going to regret it when you leave," says Elizabeth.

Later that evening, while Jewel is in the back office, she notices a chalkboard on the floor leaning against the wall. Judy drew a calendar for the 25 days of Christmas with a Black Santa Claus hovering over the calendar. Jewel calls Brenda into the back room. "Brenda, you see what Judy drew? It's a Black Santa Claus."

"No, I didn't notice it. That's interesting, I guess she wins," says Brenda. Jewel didn't think so. Jewel didn't trust any young White woman who believes they're too good of a person to speak to a Black person first. Back to work they go.

Reviews posted about Karen:

"Our vacation at the Garden Tree was a huge disappointment. We've been coming here for twenty years and always had a great experience, however, since the owner passed on the flame to his daughter to run the business, it's been downhill from here. She's super unfriendly and she's very rude to the customers. The place hasn't been renovated in years. 10 p.m. curfew is strictly enforced where you literally need to whisper if you want to talk. There are too many issues to list, so I strongly recommend not booking your stay here unless you want

your vacation ruined."

"Horrible management, I cannot put into words how astonished I am at this hotel general manager, Karen. Her lack of maturity and leadership are appalling. She's rude and she doesn't know how to communicate with the guests. If I were you, I recommend you check out other hotels in the area before you stay here. Poor leadership at the top usually signals poor service and execution throughout the hotel. If I were you I would consider other options for your stay in Lake Avid."

The negative reviews continue and continue, always directed at Karen and her poor management skills. Karen is the owner so she can run her business as she wishes! It's suggested, if you don't like her style, don't stay in her hotel.

The End

J olly is visiting her mother for the holidays. Jewel is working on Christmas Day. Jolly has arrived at the hotel. She takes a moment to look at her surroundings. Her starry-eyes are in awe of what she is seeing. The beauty of the lobby has taken her breath away. Jolly came to pamper herself at the pool, sauna, and steam room. Before she walks to the spa, she stops to chat.

"Ma what a beautiful hotel you work at!" Jolly acknowledged.

"Thank you Jolly. It is a nice view to look at everyday."

Throughout Jolly's two week visit in Lake Avid, Jewel finally introduces her to Elizabeth and Brenda. Jewel has spoken so highly of both ladies. She talks about all the healthy food Elizabeth brings her. She explains the recycling program between them with the yogurt containers. Jewel also returns all the corn husk for Elizabeth's animals.

One night, Jolly, Brenda, and Jewel go out to the local bar and have a few drinks. Brenda and Jolly really hit it off. They had a great time, laughing, talking and joking.

Jolly liked Elizabeth! She said, "Ma, Elizabeth is your friend." It was surprising to hear Jolly say that. Jolly thought most of the people around were racist.

Jolly visited the area a few times since her mother randomly decided to move to Lake Avid. She noticed the racism right away. Racist comments have been said to her by one of Jewel's neighbors. He made reference to Jewel running a slave ship in the health food store. Jewel was the only employee. When Jolly was in town, she would help her mother out. The guy was a lonely old dick. He wasn't the only dick. The neighbor next door to the health food store was a "Karen." She enjoyed talking about how much money she had. Who does that? Do you walk around telling people how much money you have in the bank?

Jolly could see the obvious beauty of the land, but she couldn't stay around too long knowing people didn't like her because of the color of her skin. Jewel could understand her daughter's feelings, even though she wanted her to stay. The time Jewel spent growing up in Long Island conditioned her to live around racism. It's a unique and unusual way to be and it's sad. However, Jewel is allowed to grow old breathing the fresh mountain air just as much as the next person. Jewel pays haters no attention. She just distances herself from them. Thank goodness Jewel felt the majority of the people were not racist in the area. There were just a few rotten apples in the bunch.

Brenda has moved on. The count down to getting rid of all the Black girls continues. Karen does a great job at representing herself as not having any racial motivations. She has her clique do her dirty work for her.

It is easy to find employment in Lake Avid. There are streets full of hotels and sport venues. Jewel posts her resume on Indeed. Indeed was a great tool to find her next job. Jewel is soon hired by the state of NY.

Jewel emails Karen that she's found new employment and December 30, 2022 will be her last day. Karen tried to get Jewel to work up to New Year's Eve. Jewel could no longer handle the "Karen" vibe throughout the hotel. And when pay day came and Becky didn't pay her for her sick pay, it was a wrap for her. Karen received another email from Jewel. The email told Karen that she will not be returning at all.

The scam worked, Becky and the company kept Jewel's sick pay. The haters around the hotel got their wishes of removing Black people in their space. See, "Karens" are always mad and difficult to please. Karen was envious of Jewel. And in addition, she was mad that Jewel wasn't envious of her. "Karen" gets super mad when a Black woman isn't jealous of them. They don't know how to handle it and in turn set out to retaliate.

Jewel will miss Elizabeth. They spent lots of time working together. Jewel loved the treats Elizabeth often brought her. She would bring all the healthy snacks with her to work because she knew how much Jewel enjoyed eating. For example, bags of mixed nuts and an apple. Elizabeth got joy out of watching Jewel enjoy the simple things in life.

While Elizabeth enjoyed Jewel's company, she was great at playing the game. She worked hard for the money she made and the less competition, the better for her. With Brenda and Jewel gone, this was the time for Elizabeth to get the money she has been asking for. She looks indispensable at the moment. This is Elizabeth's game and she's winning. She enjoys all the drama that goes on in the hotel. Her and Karen have that in common. Elizabeth is happy that Jewel's gone and has moved on to better pastures.

A special treat, an *American Greetings* card titled, "ROCK STAR, SHINING STAR, SUPERSTAR." Inside the card read, *KEEP BRIGHTENING THE WORLD WITH YOUR AWESOME SELF!* On the other side, a personal handwritten note from Elizabeth:

Jewel, I just wanted to thank you for reminding me of my self value and to never compromise. I am not going to sell my soul to the devil or Karen for a few bucks knowing the way I am treated. You standing your ground and walking out has shown me I am worth more than the Garden Tree and so are you! Keep shining Jewel, you are truly an inspiration! We are daughters of God and should be treated as such. - Elizabeth.

Two weeks after Jewel has left the Garden Tree. Elizabeth and Jewel go out for dinner and catch up. Elizabeth covers the cost. Elizabeth has grace and gratitude.

Brenda and Jewel saw each other two times after she stopped working at the hotel. Once they hooked up for dinner. And the next time they saw each other, Jewel brought the coach to the restaurant Brenda managed. A couple weeks after going to the restaurant, Jewel sent Brenda a text but she has since ghosted her. Brenda and Tanner may move on as they are known from moving from state to state. Jewel may never hear from Brenda again.

And it's okay, she found a new friend in Elizabeth.

Jewel Checks In

After spending time working as a Front Desk Clerk in a hotel, Jewel took a look at herself. Jewel judged her etiquette because some of the things she saw were nutty.

She recalled having issues with the hotel front desk staff while traveling to North Pole, Alaska. She treated herself, Nala, and her Auntie to a Norwegian Cruise. It was a two-week trip. One of the most magical places Jewel has traveled.

Disembark was in Sitka, Alaska. Jewel rented a car and they started traveling north. The trip was carefully mapped out. They stayed at a very nice Airbnb and the North Pole Hotel along the route. They traveled through Anchorage, Denali, and other places. They did all the sightseeing things you would expect to do in Alaska, by train, air, and hiking. They even saw moose walking around. The three did dog sledding rides and the Riverboat excursions, it was heavenly. They were excited when they finally reached the North Pole. Santa Claus lives in the North Pole with all his reindeer. Jewel felt like a little kid and decided to live out her fantasy to the fullest.

Nala and her Auntie are religious people of the Islamic faith. They are fully covered in their Hijab.

Auntie looks at Jewel while we're waiting in line to check

into the hotel.

"We're getting our own rooms?"

"No, Auntie, we're all staying in the same room. I got two
queen beds so you and Ma can sleep together."

Jewel could tell from the frown on her aunt's face she was
not into this Christmas themed room.

Jewel booked a Christmas-decorated hotel room in
September. It's an upgrade. They checked in the room
rather late in the evening after 6:00 p.m. They don't stay in
the room too long. Just long enough to check it out. Jewel
was excited to be living out this fantasy. Jewel's auntie is
looking at her with a side eye. She thinks Jewel's a little
nutty. Obviously, her and Nala aren't into the Christmas
fantasy. They're going along with everything to make her
happy.

They head out for dinner and return after 8:00 p.m. While
getting ready for bed, Nala can't stop sneezing. She's
having an allergic reaction to something in the room. It's
dust! The damn room is dusty as hell. By the time Jewel
heads down stairs to complain at the front desk, it's almost
9:00 p.m. She explains to the staff that the room is really
dusty and her mother is having a reaction. The lady was
kind and moved them to another room. It was a standard
deluxe hotel room, nothing fancy like the Christmas room.

"Ma'am the Christmas room was an upgrade. When should
I expect my refund for the difference?" Jewel brings to the
front desk clerk's attention.

"Yes, Jewel. You'll have to come back in the morning to speak with a manager about the refund.

"Thank you, for all your help. May I have your name please?" Jewel asked with a smile.

"Yes, of course, it's Lisa and if you need additional services please dial 0 for the front desk."

"Lisa, it was nice to meet you. Enjoy your evening."

"Thank you. You as well." Lisa says with a smile.

Jewel heads towards the elevator and gets her mother and auntie. They move to the new room. Everyone is a happy camper and slept well that evening.

The next morning, the three of them head downstairs. They're going out to eat breakfast, but first, she has to inquire about her refund. They exit the elevator. She asks her mother and auntie to sit down on the lobby's couch while she speaks with the manager. She approaches the front desk counter.

"May I please speak with a manager?"

"Yes, I'm the manager. How may I help you?"

She explains what happened with the Christmas room and how it was so dusty that her mother had a sneezing frenzy.

"You reported this issue too late in the evening; I cannot give you a refund."

"Excuse me!" Jewel's voice pitch has risen.

"You provided me and my family with a dusty room. It probably hasn't been cleaned since Christmas. What do you mean I came down too late? We got in after 8:00 p.m. I reported the issue before 9:00 p.m. If you don't refund me the difference, I will write the worst review you will ever read."

She can hear her mother and auntie on the couch huffing and puffing.

"I received the wrong information. I was told you came down at midnight and asked for a room change, sorry about this."

"The clerk from last night didn't give me a hard time. Why are you giving me a hard time now? You gave me a dusty room, give me my money."

The manager is typing (tap, tap) on her computer. "You'll see your refund within a day or two."

"Thank you!"

Jewel walks away. She and her family leave for breakfast.

Stinger

A couple of days before Jewel's birthday, Elizabeth decided to do something special. She loved to surprise or treat Jewel with little gifts. For example she'll bring her a bag of kale. Elizabeth does it to see the excitement in her face.

Standing at their station, while the ladies are talking, Elizabeth decides to put her plan in motion. "Jewel, if you could have anything in the world for your birthday what would it be?"

"Sex!" Jewel answers quickly. "But from a man, not you of course."

Elizabeth laughs. "Well, I can't help you with that."

Jewel puts her hands on her hips with a big grin on her face. Showing all her teeth, she says, "Okay. A man will do."

Elizabeth and Brenda are always making fun of Jewel. Jewel's the single person who works at the front desk. Elizabeth's been married for forty years and Brenda has been with Tanner for five years. All of the first shift has a man, even Gilligan, but not Ronnie. Ronnie has horrible social skills, he's single, too.

Jewel is doing her usual check in spill. She notices

Elizabeth isn't acting her usual self. She's whispering to other staff members, like she has a secret going on. Jewel is curious to know what is going on, but she's too busy with a guest to get involved.

Well, Elizabeth really got her this time. She sneaks off into the back room. She tells Jewel to stay in the front. She refuses to let Jewel come in the back to see what she is doing. Finally, she tells her to come back.

Jewel walks in the back room and Elizabeth screams.

"SURPRISE!"

Jewel looks around with her mouth wide open, speechless. Elizabeth had taped together a six foot cardboard statue of Dwayne Johnson. There was a bubble paper coming from his mouth and written on it said, "Hey Jewel! Happy Birthday, Babe. Enjoy your day." Jewel almost loses her breath from laughing. She laughed so hard that she had to run to the bathroom before she peed on herself. As she was running towards the bathroom, staff members are going to the back to see what all the fuss was about.

Once Jewel returned from the bathroom, a little more calm. Elizabeth walked over to her with a smile.

"I got you a man for your birthday. Happy Birthday, Jewel!"

Jewel gives Elizabeth a big hug. "Thank you, Elizabeth! Best gift ever!"

Elizabeth took pictures of Jewel and her new man. She posted the picture on The Rock's Facebook page. Go see for yourself, the funniest thing ever.

Hotel & Sports Trivia

1. Who was the 1980 USA Olympic Hockey Coach?

2. What was the final score in the 1980 Olympic Hockey match between the USA and Russia?

3. Who was the goalie for the 1980 USA Olympic team?

4. How many trees are saved by recycling one ton of paper?

5. What is the fastest growing woody plant on the planet?

6. How many trees are used to print a Sunday Edition of the New York Times?

7. On average, how many plastic bottles of water are recycled in the US each year?

8. What is the name of the garbage island twice the size of Texas off the coast of California?

9. True or False: Using bromine in a pool is less harsh and just as effective as chlorine.

Answers:

1. Coach Herb Brooks

2. USA 4-3 Soviet Union

3. Jim Craig

4. Seventeen trees

5. Bamboo

6. 500,000 trees

7. 12 percent

8. The Great Pacific Garbage Patch

9. True